OLD CRIMES

ALSO BY JILL MCCORKLE

NOVELS

The Cheerleader

July 7th

Tending to Virginia

Ferris Beach

Carolina Moon

Life After Life

Hieroglyphics

STORIES

Crash Diet

Final Vinyl Days

Creatures of Habit

Going Away Shoes

OLD CRIMES

and OTHER

STORIES

JILL McCORKLE

ALGONQUIN BOOKS OF CHAPEL HILL   2024

Published by
ALGONQUIN BOOKS OF CHAPEL HILL
Post Office Box 2225
Chapel Hill, North Carolina 27515-2225

an imprint of Workman Publishing
a division of Hachette Book Group, Inc.
1290 Avenue of the Americas,
New York, NY 10104

"Old Crimes," *The Southampton Review*; "The Lineman," *Ecotone*; "Low Tones,"
The Journal of the Short Story in English; "Swinger," *Oxford American*; "A Simple
Question," *Cutleaf*; "Baby in the Pan," *Narrative*; "Confessional," *Blackbird*;
"The Last Station," *Southern Review*; "Act III," *Narrative*; "Sparrow," *Ploughshares*.

Printed in the United States of America.
Design by Steve Godwin.

This is a work of fiction. While, as in all fiction, the literary perceptions and insights
are based on experience, all names, characters, places, and incidents either are
products of the author's imagination or are used fictitiously.

The publisher is not responsible for websites (or their content) that are not owned
by the publisher.

Library of Congress Cataloging-in-Publication Data
Names: McCorkle, Jill, [date]– author.
Title: Old crimes : and other stories / Jill McCorkle.
Description: First edition. | Chapel Hill, North Carolina : Algonquin Books
   of Chapel Hill, 2024. | Summary: "A collection of stories that take an
   intimate look at the moments when a person's life changes forever"—
   Provided by publisher.
Identifiers: LCCN 2023032948 | ISBN 9781616209735 (hardcover) |
   ISBN 9781643755984 (ebook)
Subjects: LCGFT: Short stories.
Classification: LCC PS3563.C3444 O44 2024 | DDC 813/.54—dc23/eng/20230725
LC record available at https://lccn.loc.gov/2023032948

10 9 8 7 6 5 4 3 2 1
First Edition

For Shannon Ravenel

Maybe all one can do is hope to end up with the right regrets.

—ARTHUR MILLER, *The Ride Down Mt. Morgan*

CONTENTS

OLD CRIMES

✳ Old Crimes

It was June 1999 and they were at a family inn in New Hampshire. It was not the romantic weekend spot Lynn had imagined when Cal invited her for a quick getaway between sessions of summer school. *Being together and time away*, he had said, *that's what we need, right?* Lynn nodded even though she was not feeling the togetherness at the moment, just the away, out in the middle of the woods in an old farmhouse with a prefab wing of rooms, like a rundown motel. The walls were covered in dark paneling and there was a faded floral bedspread, shades too small for the windows, and a forty-watt bulb in the one lamp on the dresser. The food in the dining room was family-style with very little choice, the room filled with trinkets and little wooden signs everywhere: *If it ain't broke don't fix it, Bless this mess,* and in the bathroom, *We aim to please, you aim, too, please.* There were tattered pinwheels in Pepsi bottles on the tables, a kewpie doll by the cash register, and things she had not seen in years, like pastel-colored rocks growing in a fish bowl, a dried-up sea monkey container, and a Cabbage Patch doll dressed up like a sailor. There were more toothpick holders than she had ever seen gathered in one place, and something about it all, the Early American décor—eagle decals everywhere—and empty bird feeders, all the *stuff,* left her feeling like life had slowed, clicking like a dying engine, and then stopped.

Needless to say they were not partying and celebrating the end of the century as Prince had promised they would be doing back in the eighties when they were kids growing up hundreds of miles apart—him in a cushioned suburban well-educated life in the Northeast where things like the right schools were always at the forefront; and her, maneuvering the backside of the Bible belt with all the baggage and guilt often inherent in that, no expectations of anything beyond high school graduation until the guidance counselor, barely out of college herself, insisted Lynn try. *You have choices,* the young woman kept saying. *You can go anywhere.*

Lynn had met Cal out in front of her dorm the day she moved in. That was over a year ago and he would be graduating soon. Although on break, both had brought a stack of books along for the weekend—he was studying to take the LSAT and she still wasn't sure what she wanted to do in life but knew he would be more impressed if she also had a stack of books. She was barely twenty and thought it was mean that her college advisor was saying she *had* to declare a major, something that he also said would affect the rest of her life. The high school guidance counselor had made it all sound so simple and it was anything but. Still, she had taken a lot of courses she found interesting, even when her grades didn't reflect it. She had taken one in forensic archaeology and another in ethics and the two together had left her thinking of all the many mysteries that remain unsolved and perhaps always will, not to even mention all that remains unknown and buried under ice and volcanic rock, in peat bogs and the greatest depths of the ocean.

On a whim she had taken a creative writing class even though her advisor kept saying that her chosen courses were not leading toward anything and that if she didn't buckle down, she would not be able to graduate in four years and her financial aid would likely not be extended. His voice sometimes sounded like a lawn mower in her head, muffling anything from past or present that sounded like a reprimand or a judgment. She had had enough reprimands and judgments to last a lifetime. Besides, she was the first in her family to even go to college, so whatever happened, she had at least done *something*. She had made *that* choice. That was what she told herself at the end of each day.

She made a B in the class—*some good ideas but nothing thought through*, the professor said—but she had continued to think about one of the exercises that was assigned at the end of the term. *Pick an object. Pick a place where that object exists. Imagine a person in that place with the object.* Then they were supposed to imagine a different person in that place with the object, and then another and another. How many variations— different characters, different situations, different stories—might evolve. It was amazing how something so simple could quickly become complicated.

She chose a belt because in her archaeology class she'd already been assigned to track something through the ages that people take for granted. At first she had wanted to do hats, because she loved hats of all kinds even though too self-conscious to wear them, and was inspired by that one famous bog body on the cover of one of her assigned books—the Tollund Man, ancient and frozen, and wearing a little pointed cap, a detail so simple and personal that it filled her with sadness—but when she began researching it all in the library, the history of the hat quickly became a lot more complicated, way more work than she wanted to do, though she never would have told Cal that. But the Tollund Man was also wearing a belt and it seemed clear that was the easier pursuit, not to mention it offered far more action than the hats would have, the word alone suggesting action. A belt could be a song or a drink or a slap. The belt: looping and connecting since 3300 BCE. Leather, suede, satin and silk, rope, brass, cord. Notched, cinched, buckled. It was a fashion statement, a utilitarian transport for tools and treasures, an object grown-ups could use to threaten children. It was a murder weapon, binding hands and feet or wrapped around the throat. A belt. A room. *Inside a room, behind a door, a man takes off his belt.* That was her sentence.

Who is the man? What is the situation? Is anyone else in the room?

Cal had already unbuckled his belt and stretched out on the bed in their tiny, dim room. *We have a commitment to be together for right now,* he had said any time there was discussion of the future. *Isn't that enough?* But she wasn't sure. She had set the clock in her head, something she did often when making a decision, giving herself time but knowing when the alarm sounded, she had to act: make a decision, leap. The clock was always ticking.

All choices have consequences, her guidance counselor had said. *It's not about right or wrong, but what's right for you.* She told herself that when the alarm sounded, she would decide. Was she just another notch in his belt? Or would they live ever after either happily or not? Would she be able to *not* get hurt? *Not* do something she would regret? *Not* be judged?

Before the conversation about their relationship, the drive had been pleasant enough, with many sights to see all along the way. They ate lunch while watching a trained bear show, which he said was unfortunate but she kind of liked but didn't say so—bears on bikes? It was impressive—and then they had spent the early afternoon hiking through a gorge formed 200 million years ago. They saw the Old Man in the Mountain, a famous rock formation like a giant man's profile—godlike—watching over the land. His profile had been on license plates for the state and storefront signs, and famous people had traveled far to stare up at or write about him.

And then they had arrived at the Tyner Family Inn and there *was* a waterfront as the ad had said, but it was a very long hike through the woods to get there. And then there was no beach or place to sit and it was muddy, bugs on the filmy surface, a martin house listing to one side, and a rickety dock, and they didn't see any other people at the pond or in the woods. Much of the forest had been clear-cut, stubs and stumps everywhere, and there were dangerous-looking spikes with yellow plastic ties, like an old crime scene. Yes, exactly like a crime scene and she said so, only to have him shake his head and sigh. "Why do you always see the worst possibility?" he said and she wanted to ask how he could *not* see those possibilities. How did he not see, but she felt vulnerable in the inquiry and remained silent.

Oh, the aching gills to live in such a pond, a slow evaporation with no rivulet leading to a better place. It reminded her of all the bog people in her book, in particular the Yde Girl, murdered and tossed away in the Netherlands in 54 BCE—her blonde hair stained red by the tannic acid. The facts: A sixteen-year-old girl—four and a half feet tall, with scoliosis—murdered and thrown in the bog. She was not far from the village. The woven sprang she had likely been wearing on her hair was wrapped tight around her neck; there were no signs of struggle, which meant the stab in her shoulder happened after she was strangled. And then she just stayed there, preserved by the bog, until May of 1897 when some men at work found her and freaked out.

So much unknown. Was she sacrificed to some god? *We're praying for a good crop so here's a dead girl.* Banished and executed because she had scoliosis? *She's not like the rest of us.* Or was it just that bad things had always happened to young women walking through the woods: *These big teeth? The better to eat you with my dear.* Dead already? *So, here's an extra stab. If I had a gun, I'd shoot you, too.* What Lynn had learned is that evil and violent things had been happening since the beginning of time. There had always been people who wished others harm. There had always been innocent people sacrificed.

* * *

"Who knew this place would be so run down?" Cal had said, but he didn't offer that they should consider an alternative and he didn't apologize for his choice, even after she flushed several dead roaches down the sluggish toilet; the only hand soap was a thin wafer wrapped in plastic that smelled of disinfectant. Now his pants and belt were draped over a chair and he patted the place beside him. She pulled her hair up in a high ponytail and stretched out, causing both of them to roll to the center of that way too soft mattress. It was hot. The wind had died and the oscillating fan provided little relief. The touch of his skin to hers was unbearable in the moment, just too hot in a room that already smelled soured and old. "Of course," he reminded her, "this is luxurious compared to where Pete and Roy are." His roommate, Pete, was in Ghana and Roy was working in a camp for delinquent kids in rural Tennessee. She knew she should admire that and she did, she really did, but she also knew so many people probably like those at the delinquent camp that she couldn't imagine choosing to be there. And was it so bad to long for things like a nice hotel with a clean pool? To dream of a candlelit, mahogany-paneled cocktail lounge with a piano player? Plump stuffed chairs and heavy cut-glass vases and fragile champagne flutes like in the movies. Or what about a balcony looking out at the sea—any sea. She worried that she was not as socially aware and involved as everyone else Cal valued in life, but she had seen so much firsthand and didn't want to look back. Had he figured this out or did he just hear in her silence an echo of his own voice?

And then out of nowhere a child appeared at the door, her yellow T-shirt smeared with dirt and what looked like catsup.

Her hair was a tangled mess. She announced that this was her birthday—June 6th—and she was six years old. *Six on six six, mama says, sign of the Debble.* She asked where they were from and how long they were staying. Were they married? Did they have a baby? Did they think they'd be eating the candy bar her mama left there by the bed? Lynn handed her the Milky Way that looked like it had been parked bedside for years, tattered wrapper and rock hard. The child ripped the paper away, one eye closed, as she bit into it and then chewed with her mouth open, a dribble of chocolate on her plump cheek. She stood admiring Lynn's red suitcase and clearly wanted a closer inspection, chocolate and dirt-stained little hands reaching all around. She said her name was Jane and her mama owned the place. "I'm Jane Doe," she said in a gruff voice and laughed; she had a wide space between her front teeth and dark brown eyes. "Like 'doe, a deer.'"

She pointed at a picture hanging on the wall beside a fly swatter and said the hunting dog in the bottom right corner was named BoBo and had eyes just like her daddy. "My daddy is nice like BoBo," she said. "He licks my hand like this," she licked the back of her own hand, leaving a chocolate stripe there. Lynn wanted to ask did she mean her dad or BoBo licked her but the child had moved on and again was touching everything. She lifted the lid of the suitcase and peered in. Cal asked didn't she need to be going somewhere but she just shrugged and shook her head and it seemed she was getting ready to get up on the bed when they heard a man's voice calling her name.

"Come here right now," he said. "We've told you not to bother people."

She put the half-eaten candy bar down on the bed and gave an exaggerated sigh, crossed eyes and tongue extended, then stomped away, letting the screen slam behind her.

"Finally," Cal said, his arms around Lynn's waist and attempting to pull her toward that marshmallow bed, but she stayed by the window and watched, the girl taking her time to get to the man standing there, hands on his hips and cap pulled low on his forehead. "Get in that house," he said and yanked her by the arm. "We're tired of you bothering people and if it happens again, you're gonna get it."

He pushed her toward the main house and then turned away, missing the way she stuck out her tongue, wagged her little hips, and then shook her middle finger at his back. Surely, he wasn't the dad with eyes like Bobo.

In a room, behind a door, a man takes off his belt. The child is waiting there in the corner as she was told to do, eyes fearful as he steps closer. *I warned you*, he says, *it's your own fault.*

No sooner had Cal dozed off, the thin sheet barely covering them, when the door creaked open and the girl popped her head in.

"Are you sleepin' in the daytime?" the girl said. "Mama says lazy asses do that. And you got no clothes on."

"Could you wait outside?" Lynn said. "I'll be there in a minute."

The girl crossed her arms over her chest and turned to face the wall. "Do you have underwear?"

"Please," Lynn said. "I'll be right out." She waited until the girl left, and then got up to dress. Cal made a noise and turned to the wall; he had a book under his arm, which must have been there while they were having sex—multitasking.

"Do you want to read to me?" the girl asked when Lynn came out and sat beside her on the stoop. She had a ragged copy of *Hansel and Gretel* and waved it back and forth and then forced it into Lynn's hand. It had a yard sale tag on it for five cents and was once owned by someone named Jeremy who had scrawled his name on the front cover in green crayon. "This is a scary one," the girl said—hair, teeth, nothing had been brushed, and she had scratched a mosquito bite to blood. "The mama and daddy loses them in the woods and they go eat candy at the bad witch's."

It was a cheap little version and Lynn changed some of the words around to sound more like the Brothers Grimm; she said they *dwelt* near the woods, and had the wife call the children's father *simpleton* instead of *stupid*. Lynn said how the witch, who first appeared as a kindly old woman, *beckoned* them closer with the promise of *nourishing* food and a place to rest, and the child stared up at her in wonder. "Their mama is mean and so is the witch," the girl said and looped her arm through Lynn's, then leaned her head on her shoulder; she squeezed Lynn's arm hard every time the witch spoke and then laughed at the end when they got away and their tired old father was happy to see them. The girl said she didn't know the witch just looked like an old woman and begged for Lynn to read it again and show her where it said that.

Lynn turned the flimsy pages, narrating along the way. She herself had never gotten over the cheap imitations of her own life, the cassette by "the Original Artists" she saved money for weeks to buy when she was eleven only to discover the terrible trick—the band was *named* The Original Artists—and their versions of all the popular songs everyone at school was talking about sounded nothing like what she was hearing; it left her feeling stupid and ashamed and angry that she had been misled. Or what about the dolls pretending to be Barbie—all the simplified, cheapened, dumbed-down versions of all the real things. The jeans, the sneakers, the backpack. She suddenly had the awful thought that some people might see her that way—some cheapened, dumbed-down version of something much better. It was times like that when she wanted to buoy herself and imagine the best, how she didn't need anyone else in her life, how she could live anywhere, someplace where no one remembered her as that girl; she could even live alone and be just fine. She could take the right courses and become something as the advisor had said—just choose something, make a choice—then she could get a job and go anywhere. Find an apartment. Live in a city.

Later, when Lynn was seated outside at one of the small oilcloth-covered tables, waiting for Cal to shower and join her, she told the woman what Jane had said about the photo of BoBo. The woman laughed and shook her head. "There's no BoBo. I buy those pictures to make it all look homey," she said. "I don't know those dogs and people from Adam." She laughed again and then lowered her voice. "And that girl hasn't got a daddy," the woman finally said. "Not that she knows of, that is, and truth is she hasn't got a mama either. She calls me Mama but I'm not her mama—just a temporary foster. And she keeps trying to call Hank her daddy and he doesn't want anything to do with her, you know?" The woman paused, twisted and reclipped her hair on top of her head. "And hell, I don't blame him. Him and me have only been going out since New Year's and if he leaves, it'll be that little devil's fault."

It was hard to tell how old she was. Fifty? Sixty? She was bone thin and her hair only had the slightest streaks of gray but her face and neck were wrinkled like someone who had baked in the sun. "I was told she was found on the floor of the Friendly's bathroom right down the road," the woman lowered her voice. "She was four by the time I got her, a head full of lice and still in diapers." Outside the window, the girl was standing in the spray of a rickety old sprinkler Lynn had listened to all afternoon, the words she had read in her book in rhythm with the sound. "I sure can't do it forever," the woman said. "Not for that little bit of money they send."

By then, Cal was at the table and they were given their choices of meatloaf or baked chicken. Green beans. Macaroni and cheese. There was only one other couple in there and from the looks they were passing between them, it was unlikely they would stay the night. Lynn heard the woman say their door wouldn't lock and when they arrived there was a child stretched out on the bed with her dirty feet on the bedspread.

"Still better than the dining hall," Cal said when the woman went back into the kitchen, and then their conversation was interrupted by that man, Hank, the boyfriend who wanted nothing to do with the child. He was once again yanking the girl's arm and pushing her toward the house.

"I told you," he said. "Didn't I tell you?"

"No."

"Don't you say 'no' to me."

"No."

"What?"

"No! No! No!" and off she went running across the yard and toward the woods and that scum-covered pond. He stopped at the edge to watch her go and then turned back and went into the room at the far end of the building. *In a room, behind a door, a man takes off his belt.* But this was a man she didn't want to imagine, the whole exercise turned dark and ominous, and even when she tried to create positive images—a happy, healthy man on his honeymoon or a tired, hard-working man craving a good night's sleep, maybe a man who loves to shed his work clothes and watch sitcoms and eat ice cream—the other thoughts crowded them out. Belt buckles as weapons, narrow belts looped over rafters, belts wrapping and binding wrists and ankles—hog-tied and thrown away.

Over dinner, Cal talked about studying for the LSAT and his upcoming trip out west with his family. He recalled the many family vacations from his childhood in this very area, nice inns and remote cabins on a lake. "Very different from this," he whispered. "My mom would die if she saw this place." He said that in a way that sounded proud—perhaps proud that he was doing something his mother would hate or maybe proud that he knew much better things and it left her trying to imagine his mother there in a world so foreign from the one Lynn knew. She started to tell what she had been reading about other than Hansel and Gretel, those bog bodies where the nipples had been cut off, which sounded like some gruesome serial killer, except that these were ancient, failed, or dethroned kings, the lost nipples signs that they had been stripped of their power. And who knew there was a time when servants had shown submission by sucking a king's nipples—*You'll be amazed at all there is to learn*, the high school guidance counselor had said. But really, was that any different from kissing a ring or kissing an ass? Going along with someone or something that doesn't feel right. If these nippleless guys hadn't been preserved all those years, would people even know they had done that? She felt some twinge of satisfaction with the thought that some day, even thousands of years after the fact, a new truth might be revealed.

"What are you so deep in thought about?" Cal asked and she said that the macaroni and cheese was a lot better than she had thought it would be, given how it looked, and then she told him about reading *Hansel and Gretel*. She was about to tell him what she had learned about the girl, but something made her stop. She didn't want to hear what he thought of the girl or her situation. She felt protective of everyone involved, especially the nameless woman who had somehow found her way in and out of Friendly's that day. Maybe she got on the highway and never looked back. Or maybe she went back to where she had always been—a choiceless place of judgment—unless some attentive guidance counselor saw something in her. Maybe she also was in a room behind a door, the clock in her head ticking.

Those were the images that stayed with Lynn. A cramped bathroom under fluorescent lighting and yellow tape wrapping cut and broken trees. A little girl licking chocolate from her dirty hand. Rooms and doors and belts. It was hard for her to remember Cal's face or hear his voice; she recalled he was tall and lean with sandy-colored hair and she knew he did get into law school but had no idea where. It was strange that she had once thought he was the person for her, and now he was lost in her memory, yet, the face of the Yde Girl was so clear, as was the Tolland Man and the threatening thoughts of her own imagination—*in a room, behind a door, a man takes off his belt.*

She thought of it all in 2003 when the Man in the Mountain fell 1200 feet from his perch, and then again on June 6, 2006 when that girl, Jane, would have turned thirteen. By then the world had seen Y2K come and go and the country had weathered the devastation of 9/11. She herself had managed to graduate in four years and had taught high school history for nearly a decade. She was married with two children, and then divorced and starting all over in a new place. Years behind her, yet she still thought of the girl, Jane, and of the faceless, ageless woman who had wandered in and out of that Friendly's bathroom; she wondered where they were. Or *if* they were.

✳ The Lineman

I am a lineman for the county.

It's true and there was a time when Pam laughed when I said that but now she just smirks and turns away; now she monitors the time I spend with Amanda and counts the days until the divorce comes through. Whenever I pick Amanda up for dinner, a wave of teenage cologne and strange hair colors, there's yet another pasteboard box or torn grocery bag Pam has left on the steps with some of my belongings—old shaving cream, single socks, junk mail. She says she can't bear to see me. We once had an old retriever mix named Teeny, who when caught spread-eagle on the living room sofa, stared into the far corner as if we couldn't see her plump body because she couldn't

see us. We laughed at it then. Even Pam, who was not a dog person and got angry about her shedding in the living room, had
laughed and marveled at Teeny's sweet passive attempt to make
us disappear.

"Pulling a Teeny," I almost said the other day when I arrived
early and caught her off-guard, my mother's old jewelry box and
a T-shirt I hadn't worn in over a decade in her hand. The last
time I tried to make light of her ignoring my presence, she said I
repulsed her. Somehow she has managed to take *her* affair and
turn herself into the victim. It's not easy to cross those lines up
but she has become a pro. I almost said that but then thought
better because Amanda was standing right there—fourteen and
so easy for me to lose right about now. Her hair had a bright
blue streak that day, like in the comic books, and her boots
looked like the ones I wear on the job.

The lines are still important, I had told Pam when it was clear
she'd lost interest in everything about me. The lines aren't what's
eating everybody up with cancer.

I love that song "Wichita Lineman" and have since the first
time I heard Glen Campbell singing it in 1968 when I was only
twelve years old. I read in an interview where the guy who wrote
the song saw somebody out in Oklahoma way up a pole working
all by himself and said it was "the picture of loneliness." That
phrase "picture of loneliness" has stuck with me all these years,
coming to mind when I see a certain look cross a person's face,
the look my mama often had when she thought no one was
watching her. I loved the song "Galveston," too, and always
pictured my sister—or who I thought was my sister—there on

some deserted beach waiting for her sweetheart to return. And now look at Glen, would you. Glen and my mama are riding on the same old dementia bus—destination unknown.

My parents were really my grandparents but I didn't know that until around that same time I heard "Wichita Lineman" for the first time. Kids had teased me about how old they were, especially at school events when my mama showed up and everybody assumed she was my grandma. My *mother*—my real mother—was my long-lost "sister" they rarely talked about. I only have brief, blurred memories of her—long, dark hair that hung to her waist, fringe jacket and purse. She had a chain she had made of chewing gum wrappers—Teaberry, Clove—and it trailed around the mirror over her dresser.

I learned the truth the same day my old man said he'd washed his hands of her. He wasn't the easiest person to live with before this, but afterward he was no more than a ghost. My first wife, Linda, who was my childhood sweetheart and best friend, was there to witness this. She was the only person I talked about it with, and I talked about it for the next twelve years in fact, right up to that moment I fucked everything up. My biggest failure will always be the way I so irresponsibly lost her. It's hard even now to understand, like watching a nightmare or Hitchcock. *Oh no, don't go there.* But I did.

One of the boxes Pam left on the steps had our first car phone. It was the size of a large shoebox and plugged into the cigarette lighter. She surprised me with it one Christmas, thinking I'd be impressed. She had just started her graduate work in a program called Communications and she laughed to say that this is what we had in common. We both worked in communications. We'd made jokes imitating Alexander Graham Bell: *Pam, come here, I need you*, I'd sometimes call from the bedroom.

Alexander Graham Bell didn't *need* Mr. Watson, he *wanted* him. "There's a total difference," Pam always said, hands on her hips. "*Need* is so desperate," she had said on more than one occasion, and I always responded by singing a line from Glen: "but I need you more than want you," and then explained to her how the line didn't work without that second part, "and I want you for all time," and that I was a man who was all about getting the lines right. I told her how my ideal position was strapped to a pole with my dangling cable in full view. How could she not laugh at *that*?

But by then, she didn't and of course that's when I knew the lines of communication weren't just experiencing a little overload or a break to be spliced. There was clearly someone else. I thought of poor Elisha Gray in that moment—competitor and first runner-up to Alexander Graham Bell, lost by a nose, otherwise we'd all be saying Ma Gray. All those years of hard work invested and then some other guy sweeps in and gets the prize.

And talk about miscommunication: Bell and Watson couldn't even agree on what was said and they were both right there. Bell reported: "Mr. Watson, come here, I want to see you." But what Watson heard was "Mr. Watson, come here, I want you."

* * *

When I was a child there was silence. It rang in my ears. My mama had a freestanding kerosene heater with a little round window like a porthole where I could look in and see the flame, and it was like looking into another world.

My daddy was eaten up with the blues—that's how she talked about it and she forgave him everything the blues had done. They shocked him back into life—just like Frankenstein she said—but he never stayed long. "At least he tried to get help," she said. "Some people's wiring is all messed up and they just let themselves go." I never stopped thinking about all that, the current, the wires, the way it was clear she was talking about her own daughter. I suspect that very conversation might've led me to where I am because I *do* know wires. I've got all the tools.

Pam's university guy—wasn't hard to figure out that connection—wears a little tweed fedora that I think looks too small for his head but for all I know that might be the style. Anywhere else somebody might beat his ass for wearing such a hat but not if that's what's been communicated is the thing to do there in the Digital Communications Department. When I saw who she was meeting up with, I remembered him well. I remembered him standing there at a party in his little tiny hat talking about this paper somebody was writing about, stuff that made no sense to me, whole lot of chatter.

My old man never hit me—would've been easier if he had. He just made me feel sorry for him, sorry that he wasn't getting his fair shake out there. Pity is the worst, right? Hate is so much easier. At the end Pam looked at me with both. You are pitiful, she said as she was leaving. Her carburetor was way off—I listened until she was three blocks away. Just you wait, I said to myself, when the blackout comes you'll be wishing for somebody who actually read the manual. I said, you'll be looking for somebody that knows how to do something.

Did I say how there used to be silence?

And now I'm wondering what people are going to do when the big blow comes, when all the lines are knocked out and the generators fail and we're turned back to a day guided by nothing but the sun and the moon. Do you know how to read a clock face? Have you memorized addresses and phone numbers? Do you know how to read a map? I ask Amanda, who sometimes listens but most times doesn't. I say how it used to be a person actually had to get up and walk to one place in the house to answer the phone, that it was tethered there to the wall with cords and a plug that slid neatly into a jack that people like me came and installed. You had to get up off your ass to change the channel, too; sometimes you had to put tin foil on rabbit ears and twist your body this way and that to pick up one of the three channels available in our area.

The phone was a separate entity itself. A station. A fixture. Not an appendage to interrupt you ten million times a day. My old mama had a chair built into a little table that was just for the telephone.

You had a dictionary on the shelf to look up something you didn't know. People had things like *World Book*—my old mama didn't have anything but *Funk & Wagnalls* and I was jealous of the *World Book* crowd. First thing I did as a married man with a baby coming was to go out and buy a set, and Pam who had just started taking classes at the university looked at me like I was a fool. "Of course you got a good buy!" she yelled, Amanda, who we just called *the baby* at the time, filling her abdomen. "It's like buying dinosaur food. Where have you been, Ricky?"— that was when she still called me Ricky which I'd been called my whole life; it was right before she got it in her head that I might fit in better if we called me Rick or even Rich or Richard. But my name isn't Richard, I told her. It's Ricky. On my birth certificate it says *Ricky* and don't ask me why my mama chose to just go with Ricky, for all I know it was because of Ricky Damn Ricardo, but that's just the way it is. Maybe somewhere out there is a guy named Ricky who fathered me but that's something I'll probably never hear about.

Where have you been, Rick? She said I had taken a wrong turn and missed the information highway altogether. And that has been her line for me ever since, especially once she went from adjunct to professor and really found her place there with the digital crowd and their little Friday afternoon gatherings at an outdoor café where they say things nobody else on the planet can possibly understand—it's the buzz in the wires and the wind up in the trees and yes, I am left behind in an expansive desert without even the poles and lines to mark the miles. And yes, that is lonely. *You have missed the information highway altogether, Rick.*

Not altogether, I told her about the same time everything blew up. I know things. In fact, I had begun following her by then and I did know things. Now I tell Amanda that she needs to learn how to wait and be patient. Be still and know. Somebody famous said that and if I still had my *World Books* I might be able to say who. *Be still and know.* Or maybe it's from the Bible—pretty sure it's either Walt Whitman, Confucius, or God. I don't google so you'll just have to take my word for it.

There was a time we had a turntable with speakers the size of small coffins. We had one phone in the kitchen and an extension in the bedroom and only had to dial five digits. I grew up with five digits and we didn't go to seven until I was in high school. The rotary made a nice sound and allowed time to concentrate between numbers, like the sound at the end of an album before the needle is lifted.

There was a time when we had silence.

It was so quiet you could hear what someone said.

"You know what we will all look like one day, right?" I asked Amanda when we were parked at Sonic waiting for our food. It was clear that she was hoping no friends saw her, the visor pushed to the passenger window, dark blue streaked hair hanging forward like a curtain. The days of her begging me to take her to Plaster Funtime or Chuck E. Cheese were way back in the rearview.

"Eventually," I said, waiting for her to look at me, her eyes the same shade of blue as my mother's, "we'll just have one long finger to push buttons and our arms and legs will start to disappear because we don't use them and the brain will dry up until it's about the size of a chicken brain with the attention span of one minute—little one-track—little tweet tweet." She rolled her eyes at me, phone there on her leg where she'd doodled all over her blue jeans in ink: a star, a flower, somebody's initials. Her phone lit up and made sounds every few minutes, until she finally sighed and said excuse her for one sec while she let her friends know why she wasn't answering. I didn't want to imagine what she was writing back to them, so I just continued my own thought of what the future might hold: single-lane highways with no place for detours or a U-turn. No place to safely break down. No way to prepare for the big blackout.

Pam communicates. She spends hours on Facebook flipping screen after screen of who's doing what to read this and that. I see her leaning in the doorway and grinning up at the phone in her hand to take a picture and change her profile. This is something she changes as often as her underwear. So and so has menstrual cramps and a migraine and fifty-three people like it. So and so wants you to know she's the best, a winner, a loser, pariah, a boozer. She likes all of that too. Hours of liking.

I screwed up in my first marriage, but when Amanda asked me about it I said I regretted doing the wrong thing and hurting a nice person, but that what I will never regret is having her and if I hadn't screwed up in my first marriage with Linda, I wouldn't have ever met Amanda's mother and she wouldn't be here. "See what people who are afraid of mistakes are missing?" I asked. "Great things like *you* and penicillin."

I could hear Pam in the next room, slamming cabinets and packing up my things. Amanda kept looking toward the noise.

Who knows if a kid takes being compared to penicillin as a compliment or not. Certainly I meant it as one. Pam's interests and obsessions have never lasted long. She's always moved around: libertarian, pescaterian, vegetarian, gluten-free. She is a lactose intolerant vegan agnostic.

I once heard my parents slamming around. I was in my sister's empty room, taking in how the wood of her mirror still smelled like those gum wrappers that disappeared one day when I was at school. Linda knew all about those gum wrappers and the fantasy I had that my sister would show up at the door one day. We sat in her daddy's Plymouth there in the high school parking lot and she pulled my head to her shoulder and whispered that she understood. She wore one of those furry hamster-looking coats and smelled like lemons.

Life is a test and I want Amanda to be ready. I say we need to be getting ready. And I'm not saying a thing that hasn't already been said. It's said, it's out there, and then all of a sudden some doctor who ain't a doctor says it and everybody nods like this is news. A stampede to hop on that wagon. Sheep led to slaughter. I pull for that wild one that breaks away, gets loose and goes out kicking like that dog who survived euthanasia, like the guy whose rope broke while being hanged. I have a fantasy where all of death row rises and busts loose. Why not do that instead of zombies? We know the names of serial killers and ridiculous cartoon politicians, terrorists and decadent starlets who have never done anything, but not the heroes—not the man from flight 90 on the Potomac passing that rope, not the man on flight 93 to

Pennsylvania who said *Let's roll*, and not the woman who lovingly raises a kid practically all by herself because her *worthless piece of shit* daughter left him behind.

I want Amanda to be the kind of girl people respect. I know what I DO want for her and I know what I DON'T want for her. Like there's a woman at work we call the littlest hooker—she's not really a midget but people act like she is, their hands dropping to hip height to show how big. She wears sandals like Caesar or Ben Hur and has a tramp stamp like a bar code, like you might scan that piece of meat and pay for what you get, dark eyes drawn out like a mean-ass Siamese cat. It would take a long time to get those lines straight and you can tell when she's been drinking because the lines waver and she misses and has a mark way too high like an accent mark like what we learned in school a hundred years ago. Her cheap outfits look like she shopped at the Dollar General and probably did, everything smelling like stale popcorn and floor wax.

I was bad for talking about her, as bad as anybody, until that one day she overheard me being told that I couldn't just pop in any time I wanted to pick up Amanda. "I got a boy," she said when I hung up and she was standing there holding a torn-edged little picture of a baby she had pulled from her ratty billfold. "I'm saving to get him back." She whispered, clearly not wanting all the boys to hear her. Maybe she was ashamed he'd been taken away from her, or maybe she thought they wouldn't keep meeting up with her after work if they knew there was a child somewhere. And in that minute my sister there on the beach in Galveston waiting on her boy from the service was gone and forever replaced by a hard kernel of a soul, paper-thin tracked-up skin, working a menial job and trying to stay sober.

The lines are amazing. I know people are amazed by all the wireless invisible stuff, and so am I, but I have to say I never got over being in awe of the real honest-to-God wires stretching across this country and around the world, those we can see and tend, those that can drop and jerk around like a snake, light up a mud puddle and fry the fragile life out of anybody.

Disasters make people appreciate what they should always appreciate anyway. The great human paradox is we're so stupid it never lasts. I said that one night at one of Pam's department parties and she said so and so wanted to know where I read that. It's not something I read, but something I said. Maybe no one thought I knew the word *paradox*. Wonder if they know the word *romex* or what to do with a voltmeter or fish tape. Who's got a butt set? That would get a laugh. The Blackout will come and what are they going to do? Does he even have a knife? I asked when she made me leave. Does he know how to fix a short? Snake a drain? Hell, does he know how to change a tire?

Once upon a time there was silence. You could hear yourself breathe.

One phone plugged to the wall and you didn't have to answer it. You didn't know who it was and they couldn't leave you a message. You could play tricks on people, call up and say all that shit like, Is your refrigerator running?—better go catch it!

Do you have Prince Albert in the Can? Better let him out! You could call and hear the sweet voice of someone you weren't ready to speak to. For a whole year I called Linda Connor's house as soon as I knew my mama was hard and fast asleep. I'd cover the mouthpiece with my hand so she couldn't hear my breath and my heart near about to pop a button from my shirt. Nine out of ten times it was her daddy all pissed off and saying he was going to have the phone bugged and I'd be locked up if they found me. Sometimes it was her brother who was the year ahead of me and a star on our baseball team and once about every twenty times it was her, like she knew these calls were all for her, because there was still a sweetness and a lilt when she kept calling out "Hello? Hello?" Her daddy joked about it at our rehearsal dinner there in the side room of Bernie's Seafood out on Highway 211. The big aquarium out front in the entryway gurgled away and someone had dropped a little bride and groom cake topper down to the bottom.

It was a small wedding in her sister's backyard; her cousin, Connie, sang "We've Only Just Begun," and then we drove down to South Carolina and stayed oceanfront for four days. Then I fucked up and we got divorced and then she became a nurse, married a pilot for US Air and had two sons. She was the love of my life and maybe still would be if I hadn't screwed up. Sometimes I think of that night at Bernie's Seafood and it's so real like I've stepped right back in. I listen, trying to hear what she's saying. She stood, a glass of pink champagne in her hand, and read a whole list of reasons for why she loved me. My old man wasn't feeling up to coming but gave me his cuff links to wear and my mama wore a dress she bought for the occasion, blue like her eyes, and when I had to move her into nursing care, it was something I folded up and kept. Pam wadded it up in one of the first boxes left out on the stoop. I saw it that day and instead of feeling angry at Pam, I heard Linda, like she was whispering over the years through the fabric. *I love him because, well, because I just do . . .*

But of course, if I went back and did it all right, was the kind of husband that Linda deserved, then I wouldn't have Amanda, and there has not been a day since her birth that I could imagine the world without her. I think of that night she came in reeking of cheap wine and reefer, and I held her hair back from her face while she retched for what seemed forever. She was crying and spitting and saying things you should never have to hear come out of your baby girl's mouth. I said, There there, honey. I said, We all got bad stuff in us and it has to come out. Go on and get it all out. People might think you can get through life without letting out the bad, but I've come to think that's impossible. Hold it in and it'll kill you.

"That's a girl," I said. "That's my baby girl." We were all still in the same house. Pam still at her *meeting*—there was always a *meeting* by the end—I said, "Baby girl, we all got to do some bad time and I'm just glad you're doing yours now, getting it out of your system. People break. All people break and the sooner it happens and you can get over it, the better, like dinging your car." I said, "I'm here."

I didn't say *but your mama is not here*, but I was thinking it. I knew what was going on long before I had proof. I'm not a fool, might not be out there thinking on the information highway with all those in the Digital Masturbation Whatever department she thinks hung the moon, but I am not a fool. I was once a cheating person. I can smell it a mile away. First time out and married, I was the cheat, and my sweet wife, Linda, was not capable of forgiving me. That's the way she said it, *I am just not capable.*

I still have all of Amanda's baby teeth tucked away. Who would think I was the fairy, but I was. We always said last one still awake or first one up has to be the fairy and that was always me. Baby teeth, milk teeth, nothing sweeter. Reminds me of milk toast and that experiment we used to do writing with milk and a toothpick and then holding it to the flame. I remember writing my sister's name and watching the letters appear. Do kids even do science experiments or magic tricks anymore? Is there any magic left?

What I did to lose Linda all those years ago was stupid. I still don't know what happened to me. It was that kind of woman men fall for all the time even though all of us in the audience are saying *oh no don't go there.* Oh no, Michael Douglas don't get with Glenn Close and Clint do NOT play Misty for me. You know the kind I'm talking about. You can smell them coming, the one who makes you know you'd have to hide your kid's pet bunny or else find it all boiled up on the stove—you know her— she likes to tell you all the girls hate her because they are jealous of her and all the men want to sleep with her. It's a big damn test and do you hear that sound, the hiss of gas, the scream of little fluffy tail, the tether to your whole life snapping?

Piece of tail is what my old mama used to say, the words like something she was spitting off her tongue. Don't you ever let me hear of you being one of those boys following those in heat like an old billy goat, sniffing the air for a ripe piece of tail. It's unbecoming and guess what it'll lead to? It leads to a boy like you with a mama too young to take care of him and having to rely on *her* mama and maybe *her* mama is dog-ass tired. We saw that nanny goat step right off didn't we? She would've let her kid die. Right? Am I right? Yes. Yes what? Yes Ma'am. There are good mamas and there are bad mamas, and you usually know as soon as it drops. Little thing hits the ground and either she's there to lick it clean or she wanders her selfish ass on to greener pastures and leaves it to die, fly glazed afterbirth she had not even bothered to lick off that small limp body. And then you've got the one who wanted her baby but it can't thrive and she stands there and licks anyway, and then holds watch and calls out a low, mournful call. Her milk sac is full and she is in pure agony when she knows that baby is gone. G-O-N-E, she spelled. Gone. *Even an old mama feels this way*, she said and gripped my arm hard. *Old mamas have feelings, too.*

One night I asked my mama what happened. I said, please tell me about her; tell me what happened and there was silence, unbearable silence.

There was a time when the world was so silent. The television people signed off and said goodnight and then there was the national anthem and static like white noise that ended with a bull's-eye there in the center of the screen and it stayed there until dawn, when everything warmed up and buzzed back into life. And you could enter a quiet house and even if that phone hanging on the kitchen wall had been ringing all day long, you didn't know it, and nobody's voice was trapped inside the receiver or in a box beside the phone to deliver messages.

The Blackout will come and they'll have to pay people like me to do things. People will cheer with the sight of big cables of wire. Tall poles the birds will light on. If the new Dark Age lasts too long, they'll all run out of money and die. The doers will rule. Skill will be the new money. The pussies of the planet our new poverty. I'll say I told you so. I'll crank my chainsaw and grab my toolbox.

There at the end, Pam trashed my old lady and then she trashed my sister and then she trashed my first wife and that's the one that got me, her sweet name coming off those venomous lips and like a snake, I struck. It was like I was watching my hand in slow motion. It went without me, like that boy shaking the branch in that book we read in high school. Thank God something uncurled my fist and opened, the sting of my open palm on her face sounding out in the night. Slap not hit. There's a difference. She took it but then recognizing the mileage to be gained in the moment, she sank to the floor and wailed like I had half killed her. Not saying she didn't have the right to react, not saying I had done a good thing. I know I had not. I didn't try to diminish what I'd done. I remained calm. I didn't push. I needed my baby girl and I knew I couldn't afford to make a move. *Amanda, come here, I want to see you.* I know that some day she may be all I've got.

Now, my mama sits there in her old La-Z-Boy and she's at her wedding, or she's at the hospital having a baby, nursing her baby, whispering nonsense. Then she thinks I'm the messenger bringing word that her daddy was shot and killed in WWI. She rubs my hands and studies the callouses there, my arms, my face. I stare into those old blue eyes, where the spark of recognition is as fleeting as a summer rain. I keep staring in and I tell her I miss her. I say, "You got room in there for me, Mama?" And she stares back lost in all the places in her head. But I keep staring in, that flicker of warm blue light I have known my whole life. I hear the humming; I swear I do. I know we're still connected but I can't for the life of me get an answer.

❋ Low Tones

When the light is just right—late afternoon, clear sharp angles—Loris Ward can look into the glass door of her shower and see a reflection of the little green house that backs up to her yard, as clear as if she's watching television. Everything has to line up just right to see it, and she has yet to figure it out. Does it come from the window or the mirror over the sink, where Alton's razor is still sitting, though he will never shave himself again. Razor sharp, that's how she would describe the image and closer than it really is, like in the car, that girl next door with her two-tone hair out there on the stoop making out with a boy who drives a truck with wheels so big, they need a ladder to get in. This is no exaggeration;

he keeps a stepladder in the back of his truck. The view is clear, but the time is limited; the sun shifts in the sky and the show is over.

They don't know she's watching, that she has seen the girl's hand there on his crotch. The girl laughs with her mouth wide open like a hyena and then leans forward, her mouth meeting her hand, the boy holding on to that spindly cheap rail along the steps. She had to look out the window to be sure the shower door wasn't deceiving her in its wavy, dreamlike, crystal-ball way. But no, the image was real.

The curtain falls, and it all disappears.

The girl has hair that looks like she ran out of money—half of a peroxide job—what Loris heard somebody call *ombre*, but at the time she thought *hombre*, and what in the hell did that even mean? She thought *hombre* meant a man—a gunslinging Wild Wild West man like what Alton might've wanted to be, or maybe that boy in the truck wants to be an hombre, who the hell knows? Children! Everybody says someday they will see everything and understand all that you do, but Loris doesn't believe that. How could they really know? How could her son even begin to know and understand and if he ever does get it, she will probably be dead or demented and what does it matter? There's so much of life she didn't know about. No one told her she'd lose her butt—where did it go? There was a time she could sit anywhere and be comfortable but now she needs to find seats that have some padding.

Hair thins and disappears, and skin sags and also thins, bleeds and bruises over nothing. Alton once said that when you get old, what's supposed to be hard gets soft and what's supposed to be soft gets hard, callouses like a goat hoof and toenails like sheet metal.

And hearing has gotten hard, a problem in her middle ear, a dark and lonely-looking place. They showed her the drawing on the wall when she went to get tested. They said that she was missing the low frequency, low-pitched sounds, male voices, rumbling engines. They say vowels are harder to distinguish than consonants. She learned that when underwater we hear through our bones, the sound is faster, but it confuses the brain and, she was quick to say, she certainly did not need any more of that. She said she guessed people are more bird than fish, that whoever has held their breath underwater and been relieved to get to the surface knows that.

No one prepares you. No one says how the one person you depend on to talk to in a day might up and suddenly get a bad illness that leaves him making hand signals and getting even more frustrated with you than he was for over forty years in the other life. The talk of him coming home has left her wondering how she will do it, or if she can do it. Could she lather his cheeks and scrape that razor in all the right places, around the mouth and up the throat? Adam's apples have always made her uncomfortable and why are they even called that? Adam's words got stuck in his craw? Sin and evil that they said was all Eve's fault? And people wonder why children get confused at church. She looked up "Adam's apple" and it said the language meant "man bump" and that it was yet another thing that got fertilized by hormones, a little cage locking in the voice box, and wouldn't it be something if they could retrieve those voice boxes from people like that contraption they collect after a plane crash. Just imagine that. Her mama had called the Adam's apple a *goozle*, a word Loris hasn't heard in a long, long time. He got choked right there around the *goozle*.

Right now, Alton's in the hospital where there are nurses and beds that go up and down, and pleasant people helping him eat and pee and not get choked; she goes and stands there every day not sure what to do, and it seems he looks at her like this is also all her fault.

That girl next door has a mangy old tomcat who slinks over and pisses in Loris's flower beds, then sashays off with a kiss my ass. Her tree peony that came with a tag saying its name is High Noon—speaking of hombres—looks like you-know-what and she's sure this is why, that old shitty cat and the deer out there creeping around at night. The catalog said it was deer resistant, but nobody told the deer and she has yet to see a big sunshine-yellow bloom like in the picture. Instead, it's dry and withered and disappointing.

Don't make me slap the shit out of you, she once yelled at their son and was sorry as soon as she said it. He was only eight, a plump sweet boy who still slept with a sour-smelling little stuffed owl she bought when he was a baby because it had big, brown wise-looking eyes just like him. She had held it up over his crib and said, *Who, who, who are you?* He laughed that sweet laugh every time but then there was that other day, and she was upset and feeling out of sorts and she screamed *Don't make me slap the shit out of you*, and that's not what she meant to say, and not who she ever wanted to be. That was not her. She tried to fix what she had done; she said she was sorry, said what she really meant was don't be like that boy next door, killing toads and things and always picking at the fly of his pants like he needed to pee or was going to expose himself. Sometimes she still cries thinking how she said all that. That boy next door had mental problems it turned out and ended up setting his grandmother's house on fire and having to be sent off somewhere. Last she heard he was still there, making brooms, and she's bought several over the years to make herself feel better even though none of them have been worth a damn if you're somebody who likes clean floors, but she buys them all the same. It broke her heart to think of that boy and their son was nothing like that. Their son was the opposite of that. He still is as far as she knows.

One night when she was coming home from checking on her husband, she saw a light out in the cemetery. At first it scared her, thinking it was somebody out there roaming around because that's where they often parked the criminal bus—that sick pale-yellow bus, like a cage for old, tattered birds whose flying days are over. A man with a rifle would stand there ready to shoot while the ones in jumpsuits cleaned up old litter out of the ditches by the side of the road. But, the next night, she saw it again and decided to get a flashlight and go out there, relieved to find that it was just a little battery-powered candle on the grave of a girl too young to have died, a girl not much older than that one she sees there in the shower door. It made that old song come in her head. *When will they ever learn?* Young girls, flowers, soldiers, all gone. So much gone.

* * *

The doctor told her last week that it might help if she just thinks that there are two Altons—there's the one who has been her dear devoted husband all these years (she didn't correct him) and there's this one who is helpless and frustrated and taking it out on whoever he can. He said it's because the cancer has possibly gone to his brain. He said there are two Altons, the real one and that other one, the shadow, the reflection. The day after the ambulance came and took him to the hospital, that girl with the two-toned hair brought her a loaf of bread and a stick of butter. My mother made it, the girl said, and Loris stood there holding that brick of hard, salty bread and thinking of what she could possibly say. We are praying for you, the girl said. And now look at her, just look! Praying indeed. Playing the flesh flute is more like it, doing things she should not be doing, right there in the picture on Loris's shower door.

There are two Altons. The before and the after. The nice and the hateful. The successful shop teacher and baseball coach loved by years and years of high school boys, a hero who took them under his big, perspired wing. That Alton is the one who tells jokes and still thinks Pete Rose needs to be forgiven and put in the hall of fame. He's the one who has gone on mission trips to help build houses for the poor. That's who she fell in love with back when she had a young shapely body and could hear a pin drop. That Alton was nice to be around, but the other Alton could say things that made her blood freeze and it had gotten harder and harder to know which one was there. She didn't tell the doctor but that *other* Alton had been around for years; she barely said *I do* and he reared his head.

* * *

I said it twenty goddamn times he said, but she hadn't heard, the low tones not reaching her brain. That's what the nice young ear doctor told Loris at her first examination. "You are not hearing the lowest registers," the doctor said, and then explained, her polished nails a shade of blue that matched her shoes. Loris had never seen nails that color and for that matter had never seen a doctor wearing such high heels, like a Barbie doll. She sat opposite Loris and showed her pictures of great big ears and explained how it all worked. "I suspect you might be missing deep voices, have you noticed this?"

Had she noticed? How could she *not* notice? Alton had told her a thousand times that she needed to get her ears examined and maybe her head, too. The young woman—an "Otolaryngologist," the paper on the wall said—explained all about bass levels, certain instruments or thunder, male voices.

"I bet you can't say your job word fast," Loris said. "I can't even pronounce it and yes, I've noticed all that you said all right." Loris asked did she think this was evolution? The woman typing up all the notes thought this was hilarious and so did the doctor and Loris found herself wishing she could spend the day with them because she could not remember when she had laughed and enjoyed herself so much. That's also who told her about ombre hair and explained that it was with an *O* and not a *H* like the cowboy. The one typing notes and wearing that cute top that looked like an animal—leopard or tiger or something—had said her daughter had come home with half her hair a magenta color—magenta ombre—and Loris laughed at that because it was before she knew it was a French word and not something out of a Western. She had learned more in that hour visit than she had learned in years. When she said that about evolution, the woman typing said, "Oh hell yeah, sister," and raised a coffee mug that said KISS MY KEISTER like she was making a toast. "No more mansplaining. Gone. Extinct!"

They showed her the devices that would help her the most—tiny little things that cost about the same as her Nissan—and she placed the order and got on a payment plan. She had the best time that day and was looking forward to coming back to get fitted, but then on the way home, her mind had turned to how she was going to tell Alton the cost. *You remember how you said I needed to get my ears checked? Wow, you were so right. Thank you! I wouldn't have known how bad I needed these things without you.* But then, she didn't even get to tell him because that was the very week that he got so much worse, not even able to swallow, and gasping for air. That was when she called the ambulance and while in the bathroom getting him a cool cloth for where he fell and hit his head, she looked in the shower door and saw the green house from next door, that cat swishing around the tires of that tall truck.

"Now is your name Loris or Lois?" A different woman was checking her in and doing all the typing this time and she was disappointed not to see Kiss My Keister.

"Loris, like that town in South Carolina," she said and when a woman sitting in the waiting area laughed, she continued, encouraged to have a listener. "Or like those little nighttime animals they keep over at the university." She turned to see if the woman would laugh again but she was staring down at a magazine. People have always quizzed her about her name and used to, it made her mad at her mama for making something that should be simple so difficult. Why not drop the R and just be Lois? Then people might say, *like Lois Lane?* And she could say something like, *Yeah but you ain't Superman.*

Alton always said, "why'd your mama put that R in your name or was it a mistake at the hospital? I bet it was all a mistake."

"You mean I'm a mistake?"

"No," he laughed. "Your name is a mistake. Your ignorant mama made a mistake." Even if that was true, it was wrong of him to call her mother ignorant and especially with their boy listening. He said, "Is Grandma ignorant?" She can see him so clear in her mind, almost as clear as that girl in the shower or that nice woman right there across the waiting room that laughed about the town; he still had that little stuffed owl and kept it by his bed—now she has it—and he was wearing that baseball jersey he loved so much—the Cape Fear Crocs—and who knows where that shirt is now. The team fell apart twenty years ago but it was fun while it lasted, fun to go and sit outdoors and listen to people talking and laughing, Alton explaining every play whether she wanted to hear it or not and their boy out there with his face pressed to the fence hoping to speak to a player. She loved those ballgames, the sounds, the sunsets. She loved sitting beside Alton and all the people who waved when they passed by, thanked him for his good work.

"I was named for the town," she told him then and a million other times.

"Well," he laughed. "She could've done better by you than Loris, South Carolina."

Loris told him how her parents named her that because they had met there in Loris at a lunch counter where they both ordered chicken bog; they always told her how if not for them being hungry at the same place at the same time, she wouldn't exist. She liked that story as a grown woman, but as a kid, it scared her to think how easily she might not be here, like if one of them had decided to go to Watson's Diner or just eat at home instead. She also thought how she might just as easily have been named Myrtle since they were right there at the beach and she thinks Loris is a hell of a lot better name than Myrtle and especially after she learned about the other Loris, those little slow-moving creatures with the great big eyes that stay up all night like her. Now, Loris is the chicken bog capital of the world with a whole celebration and everything.

Loris noticed while waiting for her appointment that the woman who had laughed was wearing a fashionable chain belt kind of like one she had long ago that had gotten away from her, but no, on second look, she saw that it wasn't a belt at all but a plain old chain, her wrists crossed in front and bound together, and there was a large woman with a gun strapped to her belt sitting beside her. That's when Loris noticed there was another woman with a gun as well. Two armed guards and a woman in chains right there in the waiting area of audiology. The woman with the chain wore a pink sweatshirt with blue flowers and had neat gray hair. She looked a lot better than the women with guns. She could be Loris's neighbor or their son's old elementary school teacher, their doctor. What on earth did that woman do? She wore sensible shoes, like a pair Loris had tried on just last week at that big shoe store near the interstate. Nice shoes, stylish and not cheap at all, which is why Loris ended up not getting them, but the woman's feet were chained, too. What on earth?

"Brenda?" The woman at the desk opened that glass slider and called out, and the woman in chains said "here" like the roll was being called, and several, Loris included, laughed.

After a moment's hesitation, Loris moved to a seat across from the woman. "I can't help but ask," she finally got up the nerve to say. "But, what on earth did you do?"

"You couldn't help asking?" The woman turned in her chair, those guards reaching for her armpits to get her to stand up but she shook them off. "Really?"

"Well, actually, what I really meant to say was I like your shoes and that I almost got myself some in navy." She gripped the arms of the chair and studied her hands, surprised by how old they looked. "I wanted to ask if they're comfortable because I know they cost a lot." Loris looked up then and studied the woman's face, so familiar. "You just don't look like a person that would be chained up."

By then, one of the guards had motioned for Brenda to get up. She was average height and weight just like Loris, probably even the same size shoe. They could have been related. "How sweet of you," she said and smiled, then she shrugged off the guards and stood a little straighter. "But that's what happens when they get you for *murder.*" The word rolled off her tongue like a long purr and then she cackled the way people do when they try to sound like a witch. It was clear she had done this before and the look the guards gave one another said it all. "And I got these shoes in the mail from somebody I know trying to *do good*, somebody who should've *done good* when I needed help, you know?"

Loris nodded—she did know—but Brenda kept right on talking. "Now these two," she swung her head back and forth, motioning at the guards. "These two love their time together. I'm the chaperone while they lovey-dovey it up in the front seat." The guards smirked at one another and sighed, one was still holding her *People* magazine bent back to a story about those people with hair to their asses who can't stop having babies, but that guard woman had almost no hair, shaved up the sides like Alton wore his, and her big black shoes splayed out like a paper doll. Loris hadn't thought of paper dolls in ages. She had made her own and even though she was a little old for it all, she loved Betsy McCall and somewhere still had a whole shoebox of all the Betsy's she had carefully cut from magazines and mounted on cardboard from the cereal boxes, the little dresses held on by fragile little paper tabs she had had to retape a million times.

"But lovey-dovey can turn on you," Brenda continued, "Am I right?" She took her time moving toward the door, staring at the people in the waiting room: a child crying on her mother's lap, an elderly couple dressed in matching purple shirts, the old man with his ears bandaged up like a dog after getting them cut. *It's called docking*, Alton once told her, and defended the process of chopping off tails and ears that she thought was so cruel.

"And, since you couldn't help asking," she said, "I killed my husband."

"Oh my," Loris said, aware that everyone was listening, or straining to listen, given where they were. "I'm sure you didn't mean to."

"Oh, I meant to all right; it was a brilliant plan and he never saw it coming. You might've read about it."

Loris leaned forward, eager to hear more. She wanted to learn more and read about it. The guards had clearly heard this before, too, and now the one with the magazine was shaking her head in disgust as they pulled her forward. "I'd tell you more but I got this appointment and these mean fat asses here are hurting my arms. I don't even know why they brought me because I'm better off *not* hearing. You know?"

Loris nodded because she did know. She did know the calm comfort of absolute silence and how hard it was to find that these days, that kind of silence like when your ears were under the water and you heard your own heart.

"Do you know what you hear at night in prison? Do you?" She stared hard at Loris and then looked around the room again, her look lingering on the child who now was just sniffling with a thumb in her mouth. "Do any of you know what a prison cell sounds like at night? Forget how it smells, and it makes no goddamn what shoes are on your feet either. You can't have laces and you can't have a belt, not a garter belt—remember those? Not a Kotex belt, remember those?" She paused, turning back to Loris like she wanted an answer, and Loris nodded. She was old enough that she did remember both of those things. People thought garter belt and thought that was something that might get somebody worked up like those silly children throwing them around at weddings, but the one Loris had looked like a hard white girdle with straps hanging off of it, and those damn Kotex belts cut into her back with those sharp silver clamps.

"I hated those," Loris said.

Brenda smiled, ignoring the young doctor there at the door waiting for her. "So did I, but what I wouldn't give right now for a big ugly purse full of Kotex pads and cigarettes and cheap lipstick. I had all that—I had right much in this world and then poof, all gone, just because there's always some nosy-ass witness looking out a window or hearing something in the middle of the night to mess it all up."

Loris wanted to ask what that man did to make her kill him; she bet he might've knocked her around or maybe he kept old smutty books under his mattress but called her a rotten whore if she tried to be exciting like somebody in a movie; maybe he put on a good show for everybody in the world but her. Maybe Brenda had done everything in life she possibly could and had run out of choices.

The woman at the desk called Brenda's name again and the guards tugged her over to the door where the young audiologist, or whatever that other word was, was waiting with a smile and a clipboard. One of the guards said, "Show's over, Brenda."

"Think what you want, Fido," she said. "You can do a lot of things but you can't chain my brain." She laughed and turned back one final time. "I like your purse, by the way." Brenda nodded at Loris's bag there on the floor by her chair and Loris smiled her thank you. She liked it, too, and had gotten a good price at T.J.Maxx; it was part leather—the strap and the trim—and once cost four times what she paid. "I sure miss having a place to hide things."

The first time Alton ever slapped her in the face was one night after they went to the movies. It was after they saw *The Poseidon*

Adventure, but then it seemed like a slap or two became the price of the ticket. A night in the cool dark with some popcorn and a big soda, him holding her hand and squeezing during the scary parts, seemed to lead straight to that other Alton, and she has yet to understand why. Was it that she enjoyed herself and felt so good she said more than she should have? Or did seeing a world beyond the one where he was the star turn him hateful? Once, on his birthday, she surprised him when they went to see that movie *The Sailor Who Fell From Grace with the Sea*. She thought it was going to be about sailboats or maybe a fishing trip and he liked that sort of thing. She had baked a cake for after they got home but she still went all out and bought popcorn and Milk Duds. She had no idea it was going to have that scene of Sarah Miles there on the big screen working herself up not unlike what might be happening with those children next door right this minute for all she knows. That boy's truck is parked on the street but it's cloudy and all she can see of the house is out the window so who knows what is going on over there while the girl's mama is at work. What happened to Kris Kristofferson in that movie is too awful to even think about, those mean children acting like he might be a surgery experiment. The ad had said "He gave his soul to the sea and his heart to a woman" and there was a picture of Kris in bell-bottoms, handsome as ever, so how in the hell did she know what was going to happen. *Damn Almighty*, Alton had said. *What in the hell are you trying to do to me, woman? What in the hell were you thinking?*

Well, who knows what she was thinking but about going to the movies and trying to have a nice time out for his birthday, but what she does know is that one day she is going to walk over there and let those children know what she thinks. She is going to catch them off-guard, a day where the grass is wet and she won't crunch the leaves. She learned that from listening to Alton and his hunter friends. She knows how to be very quiet when she needs to be, quiet like a hoot owl, slow and silent.

There's a pond not far down the road, there near the cemetery, and it's where Alton used to go fish all the time. She went every now and then, when she thought she wouldn't get eaten by mosquitoes or black flies. One time—the water unusually clear after days and days of hard rain, she would have sworn she saw the outline of a truck down below the dark waters. She thought of it not long ago in fact, back when the hurricane came through and that Jim man of the weather station was in a rowboat coming through a neighborhood where she had roller-skated as a child, cars and houses way down below like one of those globes you shake up.

Even scarier, it made her think of *The Night of the Hunter* with poor Shelley Winters drowned there while her murderer, that hateful Robert Mitchum preacher character, went riding off whistling a tune, his fingers tattooed to say LOVE and HATE. Shelley Winters also nearly drowned and then died in *The Poseidon Adventure* and Loris loved that song "The Morning After" and how that night at the movies was a good one, holding Alton's hand during the suspenseful parts, sharing popcorn; their boy was in high school at the time and doing so well. She was so proud of him and even though Alton slapped her at the end of it all, she still had enjoyed being at the movie and if she heard that song right now, she would think of their old green Impala with that playing on the radio.

Alton had said Shelley Winters needed to stay away from the water, which made them both laugh. They were walking arm in arm to the car when he said it and it felt so good to laugh and then Loris remembered that something about water and swimming also came up in another old Shelley Winters movie, *A Patch of Blue*, where Shelley plays the hateful mother of a sweet blind girl who sits in the park stringing beads. That was an old one, Shelley quite a bit younger, and Alton said what he remembered is that he hated that movie because it was pitching something that went against what he believed in. He didn't think that blind girl had any business being friends with Sidney Poitier, period, only he didn't call Sidney Poitier by his name. They were still arm in arm and Loris said that she liked Sidney and had read in a magazine where he was married to a beautiful white woman; then she said how she bet he made more money in an hour than they'd see in years and before she could even finish, his open palm came across her face. Nobody saw that happen. If there was a witness, someone looking from a window somewhere, it was never told, and when they got in the car, he said he worked too goddamn hard to hear such a thing from her. What did she do after all? What in the hell was she thinking?

When she said she thought she saw a truck down deep in that pond, Alton said it had been down there forever, that somebody once told him what happened but he forgot the details, bad brakes or something like that. But she thinks something else, always has, just like she knows those children next door are up to no good. Sometimes she opens the linen closet or his chest of drawers and she expects to find something. And yes, she watches too many movies, but lately, she feels that way a lot of the time, his belongings making her more and more uncomfortable, that razor and his big tool belt, that magazine that comes in brown paper she burns in the fireplace and that other one, *American Rifleman*. At first, she thought it was like that TV show they used to like starring Chuck Connors—gun-slinging hombre—but no, it was page after page of weapons with names: Hellcat and Python, Little Hot Shot, Golden Eagle. She wondered did those guards have guns with a name that came with them. *Silencer Central delivered right to your door* it said on the cover near his name and their address.

Silence. In a way she hadn't even noticed her hearing loss, hadn't really minded the muffled sounds like being underwater, like now, looking in the shower door where life turns wavy and it's hard to know what's real. Everybody in town loved Alton and praised his work. That Alton, what a great guy, Mr. Shop who helped so many young men find their way. They called him a master carpenter, Jesus's helper, Bob Villa in the later years. *Aren't you proud?* people asked, and she said yes but their son said *no*. He told her things Alton had said or done but it was hard to hear. He said, *Why are you still there, Mom?* He said, *Do you hear me?*

Their son dove down in that pond once. He wore a mask and flippers and reminded her of a frogman or like Lloyd Bridges in

Sea Hunt, another show she had liked to watch and certainly Lloyd seemed like a good role model, and it seems his sons have turned out real good; Loris has seen them in a movie or two, one especially has gotten a lot of attention and she is sure Lloyd must've been proud as long as he lived. But, that day at the pond, their son came sputtering up to the surface and said he had touched the roof of the truck, had felt around enough to know the windows were cracked open several inches. Alton rushed forward to call him foolish—*goddamnit*, he said. Alton stood chest deep in the mossy water and screamed for him to get the hell out of there before a moccasin got him. "You could have drowned down there or gotten bit," he said, fist curled like he wanted to hit, sweat on that bloodred face.

Now their son is in Alberta, Canada, and sent her a beautiful photo of his wife and two kids. He wrote her about snow and clear cold lakes and a place called Peace Park, which sounds so nice. *We have room for you*, he said several years ago, but when she mentioned Alton, he said nothing and now his letters are short and like something out of a travel book—the leaves are turning, the nights are cold, hope you are taking care of yourself—and she hasn't seen a photo in over a year.

If that was her son over there at the green house with the girl with ombre hair, she'd go over and have a word with him. She would creep up silently and surprise them, but she would never do what Alton did; she would never chase and hit him so hard he had to miss school, and if she could take back something in her life it would be that time she told her son she was going to slap the shit out of him. She wouldn't have done that. She knows that even at her maddest, she wouldn't have done that. She would never have done that and she would never have done what Alton did—that belt of his—she hated that, the sound, the hard exhalation coming from their boy's lungs—and where did that belt go? She asked one day, where'd you leave your belt? That one with the big hammer on the buckle, and he blamed the boy. He said their boy stole and hid it so he wouldn't get what was coming to him. He said that boy is full of shit if he thinks that's gonna change anything. He said, *C'mon, boy, tell the truth, be honest for once.*

"I didn't steal your belt!" he said. "I swear to God I didn't and I also know nothing will keep you from doing what you want to do." His plate of half-eaten food sat cold in front of him. She remembers the field peas she had shelled herself. She remembers those little Jiffy corn muffins she used to make all the time because their boy loved those and liked them at breakfast, too. Sometimes she put one in his lunch he took off to school. "Mom, you believe me, right?"

She wanted to believe him; she did.

"Mom!"

She wanted to believe him. She wanted to.

Just last night she went and slipped down the hospital hall so quietly. It was unusual for her to go that late; it was already dark because the little light in the cemetery was glowing from that grave and just the sight of it had put that song in her head again—*Where have all the flowers gone? The young girls and the young boys?* The nurse was surprised to see her there and held a finger up to her lips to be real quiet. She entered his room without making a sound. She could see him in the mirror, eyes staring up at the ceiling, cheeks hollowed out and gray with stubble, mouth hanging open and oxygen in his nose. She held her purse that Brenda had complimented in front of herself like a shield and inside was the card her son sent a few weeks ago. He said whatever happened, he would not be coming home. He wrote: *That ship sailed long ago.* He wrote: *Take care.*

She would rather look at Alton in the mirror than Alton in the bed. Alton in the bed looked her way and reached his hand out but she stepped back, out of the image in the mirror and into the darkest corner. Then it was just him all by himself in the mirror. *Who are you?* She whispered. *Who? Who?* He opened his mouth like he wanted to say something but there was no need, and she said as much, then pulled her purse close to her chest and slipped from the room without a sound. She didn't need any words because she could see it all so clearly, like a silent underwater movie.

✳ Commandments

We met once a month, a self-help group of sorts, and had for over a year. What we had in common was the man who had wooed, captivated, and then cruelly dumped us. We joked that we were bound by rage and regret—our barbs and revenge plots worthy of a movie script—and we always arrived with gossip to tell or witty, well-rehearsed lines. It was easy to find one another in our university town, as well as this place we heard he now liked to frequent, a tiny out-of-the-way café.

These days the café boasted something for everyone. "The boss wants to bridge the gap," our waitress said and smirked when we expressed surprise over the menu. "Carnivore and

Crunchy, come one and all." She rubbed her fingers suggesting money. "Meanwhile, he thinks it's fine to make us wear name tags with names that all sound sweet and edible." She had waited on us many times—ponytail, scaly reptile tattoo climbing her leg, big dark eyes that always looked surprised—and we often lowered our voices when we saw her coming because she liked to join in the conversation. She also worked as a dog walker and more than once had come to take our order with a roll of poop bags hanging off her belt. Her name tag said CANDY and she had told us that unlike the other servers—Taffy, Brandy, Shug, and Honey—her name really *was* Candy. On the birth certificate: *Candy.* And not Candace or Candide or even Canada, and she was planning to rename herself, high on her to-do list along with finish school and get a good job by her thirty-second birthday, which was coming next year. We had asked if she wanted us to call her something else, and so far she had toyed with Gwendolyn, Victoria, and Veronica. She said she wanted something long that would leave lots of options. "I feel it's my turn to have some options, you know?" she asked, and we all nodded. "Like I've had enough shit in life and I'm ready for something good."

She was studying to teach health and PE, and she swore that once she graduated she would never darken the doorway of that restaurant again. She was a walking dispenser of tips and advice, whether asked-for or not, and had given her thoughts about what stilettos did to your feet (nothing good) and Spanx to your circulation (suffocation, camel toe, and muffin top) and how we needed to drink water all day long ("pee clear and you will see clear"). When she heard a fact or piece of advice that would make her life better, she had it tattooed on her body. That day, she had pulled up her sleeve to show *water, water everywhere.* She said she forgot who said it but it had been stuck in her head like an earworm since the tenth grade when her teacher read it aloud to the class. "Most of it was about a stinky dead bird, but what I remembered was water. 'Water, water'—flush your system, saturate your skin, you know?"

We had yet to see the man who had dumped us, but the day would come. He liked to be seen and he clearly liked his reputation as a ladies' man. He was one of those guys who had perfected the art of ruining women, always going for the brightest and best, the girl most treasured by everyone around her, only to then, over the course of several months or a year, reduce her to her lowest common denominator, someone lacking self-confidence and losing the shine that originally drew him to her in the first place. Perhaps it was not even a conscious thing, this knack he had for discovering a woman's greatest vulnerabilities and then playing on them enough to peel her down to her weakest, thinnest self. And of course, then why would he be attracted to *that*—dry skin and straw hair and limbs like toothpicks—when there was a new one in the brightest corner?

"Who does he think he is?" we mused after some therapy and gaining back the pounds and self-esteem lost during his monitoring and judgment. We came out of it as if we had been drugged, helpless, and our time with him was some sort of altered state. We felt ashamed that we had been there but even more so that we were the losers, because we had all gone in thinking we would be the *one*, the victorious presence that would bring meaning to his very successful but emotionally empty life.

He was not even a handsome man, at least not classically so; feature by feature he was pretty average looking—high forehead, hazel eyes, slightly crooked nose; he claimed high school sports, but we later learned a speed boat accident and not even one of great daring, the boat took off and he wasn't paying attention. His lips were just full enough to suggest a kind of pensiveness but nothing so special. It was said that as a frat boy in some big Southern school his hobby was rating women as they passed by, holding up cards with numbers and shouting out nicknames. One of us knew this firsthand from someone who had allowed an extra fifteen minutes to get to class for fear of having to walk that way. Did anyone say, *Oh, but he was just a boy playing a little game.* Probably. Did we say how we all outgrow things? Ask who wants to be held accountable for all the dumb things done in youth?

And he had grown up to do very well in the world. He carried himself like some kind of god and exuded a charm and confidence that made people want him on their team, at their party, in their neighborhood. They wanted his fat wallet and extensive network. *Had we?* He baited and secured his hook in the most subtle ways and then listened to intimate confessionals without even asking; he knew the power of attentive silence, and we over gave of ourselves, preparing the cold ground for his big thaw.

We were kind of a First Wives Club, though of course, none of us had been married to him. Only one had even hit the year mark, and yet, the damage had been done. We'd started meeting out of vengeful curiosity that we called self-improvement to discuss and compare what we had endured during *our time*, words spoken with grave distinction, though all the stories sounded pretty much the same. The adoring nonstop attention: the steady pressure to distance ourselves from our family and friends, to be more independent; then the shift to withholding information and affection. We spoke with a kind of bitter envy about whoever was his latest, *that poor fool, we don't envy her,* and yet there was also a level of distrust among us. Would we go back if given the chance? Time had allowed us all a resurrected bit of strength so that if we got a next time, things certainly would be different, but now, thankfully, we had other lives. Still, we could imagine teaching him a thing or two—or even better, we sometimes imagined he had already learned and seen his great mistakes.

We had each been told by reputable therapists that this was foolish, self-destructive thinking, and maybe that was another thing that held us together—we urged each other on anyway. We went where the therapists had refused to go and continued to beat that decayed horse down to the bare bones. I shared how my therapist had lectured me that just because someone had money or a good job did not mean that they were free of sociopathic tendencies, but when I let his name slip, her cheeks flushed and she stifled a cough, took a long drink of water, and said *oh really,* then fidgeted with a corner of her legal pad the rest of the time.

We had even talked about the sex, feeding the myth far more than it deserved to be fed, and telling details no one should tell. It was a poker game of sorts, and though sometimes we really *wanted* to show our hands in the name of womanhood— kindred sisters—none of us ever did. We could all describe his condo on the coast, the king-sized bed with a view of the ocean, those quiet moments while he was still sleeping beneath that heavy gray linen comforter. We all remembered early morning darkness staring out at the stars and the stillness of the beach below, soothed by the sound of the surf and the white noise he kept running in every room. The walls and rugs and shades and furniture were like a black-and-white film and we had all—on the best days—felt indispensable and important; we were the pop of Technicolor that his world needed—a tangerine cashmere sweater left folded over a chair, peacock blue scarf, plum silk camisole.

We had all had an exciting early date that resembled one of those reality shows. One flew to Maine for lobster, another to see the Northern Lights. I went to Bermuda because I had asked if the sand was really pink. And he had talked about the future to each of us on those trips: wouldn't it be wonderful if we could just stay right there forever, he liked to say, you could just quit your little job (in our case this would be teacher, orthodontist, interior designer), but we'd have to watch the children so close to the ocean. *We? Children?* Was I the only one who heard those words? But no, we each had been introduced to our imaginary children that shared our interests and his face. Now it was comical to think about, these fantasy families in those concocted lives.

Bullshit! We screamed and poured more wine. *What were we thinking?* And why was it that none of us actually knew what it was he did? Was he even legit? This big fish in the designated pond always working to stay in the good graces of the many names he dropped of those with money and power? Did we even know how he voted?

"That's a bad sign," Candy, somehow carrying three trays and a bottle of wine, said in passing.

The women in his life changed, but as far as we could tell pretty much everything else remained the same: name in the news as often as he could swing it, photos of him in first-class seats at big sporting events and charity events, presenting the trophy at the golf tournament he sponsored, and all the wives of others too old to catch his eye (fifty and up) who talked about how wonderful he was and how surely one of these days he would meet Mrs. Right. None of that had changed, including the mysterious housekeeper who pretended she spoke no English.

Is he home? (huh?) *Did he say where he was going or when he'd be back?* (huh?) *Did he leave any messages for me?* Shrug shrug—the tangerine cashmere, peacock blue scarf, plum camisole handed out the door. But one of us, still secretly cushioned in the cool, carpeted upstairs, had once heard her rant—a deep, low country twang punctuated with a smoker's cough. She'd slammed the door and said how one day it was gonna be a husband with a gun and more power to him, she was sick of that shit and as soon as she finished paying her kid's tuition, she was quitting.

He had told us all that he had a terribly traumatic childhood but with no details. He said it was all too hard to even think about; he said, no one would believe all that he had endured in life. He used the word *trauma* a lot. He said he couldn't afford to look back. He always squeezed his eyes and fists when he said this and that vein up in his forehead buckled a little. He said what he loved about us was how kind and understanding we were of his pain.

"Well, that's still no green light for being an asshole," Candy said. She stood there tapping what looked like a combat boot, that scaly snake or lizard tattoo climbing up her leg. "Sorry for eavesdropping but hard not to hear you guys. You know? *Be ye not an asshole* was one of my first tattoos."

We reminded her that we were there for lunch and maybe she could take our order. She grinned a great big fake smile, assured us of her perkiness, and reeled off the specials. "I say all that," she added at the end, "But I'm not sure why because you three get the same salads every time—California Cobb, Crispy Kale, Pesto Pasta. That one gets chamomile tea now that she's pregnant and you get the cabernet, and she gets the pinot gris—nobody eats dessert even though you think and talk about it for a very very long time even if there's a line out the door waiting for a table." She capped the pen and did a little curtsy. "Oh, and you always round up to dollars on an already generous tip, which is greatly appreciated."

There were many good reasons to quit the group—we all were in new relationships—but by then, we had formed a genuine camaraderie and were addicted to the rehashing. It was fun to track him—a game of sorts and so easy to do, as successful and prominent as he was. I secretly still had him on Google Alert (for the group, of course), and what would he think on that anticipated day when our timing was perfect and there we sat, ghosts of his past. We had rehearsed what we'd each say many times—"Well fancy seeing you here, put on some pounds haven't you?"

I had started our little chain—a few women refusing to respond to my calls, and no doubt there were many we didn't know about. We had heard that lately he was seeing a local musician who was as young as legally possible, and we had made bets on when *she* would look in the mirror—ego shattered—and hear him say, *What's your fucking problem?*

We had been staring at a photo of that young singer in the community entertainment rag and it was hard to imagine she could get any skinnier and still be alive and there was no way you could ever detect dark circles given the eye makeup she already wore. She had dyed black hair and ripped-up fishnets and an expression that looked like she was in great pain. We thought she looked like part of the Addams Family or Elvira, Mistress of the Dark. She had a safety pin in her nose and her ear lobes were stretched in a way that made us all wince to see. Was this a costume or did she always look like this?

"You guys listen to her?" Candy laughed as she refilled our waters.

"No, do you?"

"No, too boo-hoo emo for me, you know? But why are you talking about her? I mean sorry if I'm butting in, but this is too much." She shook her head. "You're always the loudest table in here. In a good way, of course. Are y'all like a club or something? I've always been meaning to ask."

We finally caved and told her the reason we had begun meeting in the first place and why we were looking at the photo of that young singer. We owed her our story, given all that she had chosen to share with us about her own life and her name and her problems with her mother, who thought tattoos were obscene. She had told us about her dad who had introduced her to the early SNL reruns when it was just the two of them watching and then who died way too young when she needed him most, and about her desire to have a baby in the future, with or without anyone in her life. One day she had told us that she was considering the sperm bank, that she knew someone who had studied that catalog of donors the way her old grandma had talked about the Sears wish book that came when she was a girl, and that there were some very impressive choices. Then she had heard the owner of the restaurant telling how when he was in school and a struggling student, he sold his plasma and sperm as often as they'd let him. "God," she had said. "So, imagine like that scary old movie *The Boys from Brazil*, only instead of looking like Hitler, they're all ZZ Top like the owner, long beards and craft-beer bellies." She made a face—wrinkled nose and crossed eyes—the same face she made when we told her about the man we all had in common.

"You mean that old guy?" she said—talk about being loud—water pitcher poised in midair. "The creepy old guy always talking about his Tesla and his season tickets to everything and his stocks?" She shook her head and wiped tears from her eyes, put a finger in her mouth and did a pretend gag then looked like she was about to pull up a chair. "He's been coming in here forever, right, or at least while I've worked here, told me he had invested heavily in this business and needed to check on things." She snorted again and shook her head. "Is that who *I'm so Miserable, I might slit my wrists* is with? She can do better than *that*. Maybe she's looking for more reasons to be miserable and God only knows what he's looking for, a pulse maybe, no offense." She studied our designer clothes and purses and smirked again.

"But you know who he is, right?" we asked. We said his name and she blinked and shrugged, no recognition other than he was the *creepy guy* who liked to sit off in the corner, who never rounded up the tip, leaving only 10 percent on the nose, pennies on the table! Drank martinis straight up and had a weakness for Tater Tots. "I mean Tater Tots and a shitload of salt so like, who's sophisticated?" We told her how he was always in the *Wall Street Journal*, that there was once a whole spread in the *New York Times*, that he'd written a book.

"Oh, everybody's writing a book," she said, "or doing a podcast. Talk about an epidemic. Taffy, who is really Rhonda, said he once told her if she had a little work done, she could go anywhere. *Work!* He meant buy some boobs, suck some fat out of her thighs, redo her face. Around here, we call him *the creep*, or that's the polite version. He's even worse than Sanford over there, who comes in every day trying to pick up somebody." She pointed at a man in a leather jacket and Yankees cap sitting alone, who waved and grinned when she looked in his direction. "People say he's never been the same since he fell off a motorcycle, but who knows. It's sad if that's true but it doesn't make me want to date him, you know?" She stopped then, leaned in and whispered. "He—like your old dude—tries to go after people too young to know better. So, what's his book anyway, *How to Be an Asshole?*"

When she saw us eyeing her tattoos, she told us that along with the dragon on her leg and tips and advice of how to make life good, she had quotes from books she liked. She told us how on her back was a picture of her grandma, the one who loved the Sears wish book, an old country woman who used to always tell her *pretty is as pretty does*. She laughed and raised her sleeve to show the words. She said the tat artist who did her grandma's picture, though, was just getting started and so her grandma looked more like Mr. Spock. Her last guy said it scared the hell out of him if he woke up and she had her back facing, but her new guy think's it's kind of funny. Still, when she has money to spare—*right? like in a hundred years, Haha*, she said—she probably would see if the artist could change it into something else. "Like maybe a prehistoric cave," she said. "Or maybe the night sky with some stars."

She said it can be hard to cover things up, but she'd done it. An old boyfriend named Ed had become *don't be mislEd*. She said when she was growing up, that she loved the Cosby show, wanted to be a Huxtable and always pretended that Theo was her brother, and they did things together like she helped him with his homework and he complimented how smart she was and Denise always wanted to borrow her clothes and she really got tired of that. She said her mother hated that she wanted to be a Huxtable which made her want to be one even more—what kid didn't want to be a Huxtable? And so as soon as she was legal, she got a little anklet tattoo that said *every closed eye is not sleeping and every open eye is not seeing*. "Can you even believe Cosby said that? Like I thought it sounded like a wise dad kind of thing, and now it's just creepy and fucked up. I went straight and got a flower ring tatted all over it."

After she brought our cappuccinos, she continued to linger, still in disbelief that any of us had gone out with the *old creep* in the first place. "The tat artist said this poet who killed herself long ago said if the body is a temple, then tattoos are the stained-glass windows. I love that but you should have seen my mother's face when I told her, *Miss I Know God Better than Anybody.* This is the first tattoo I ever got." She pulled up the sleeve of her left arm: *After all, what's a life anyway? We're born, we live a little while, we die.* "Charlotte in *Charlotte's Web* said that. And then how about this." She pulled up her shirt for us to see the words running around her waist like a belt, her pierced navel like a sinkhole at the end of it. *People are very gullible. They'll believe anything they see in print.* "Isn't that funny? That's from Charlotte, too, and I wanted you all to see it, so you'll remember next time you read things about the old creepy guy." We looked at one another, seemingly in agreement that we would just let her keep talking. "I love that book. It changed my life and so did the librarian at my school who read it aloud to us when I was a kid. Maybe I should have inked her face somewhere! But here's what I want to tell you." She looked around to see if anyone was looking, then shrugged, took off her apron and pulled up a chair.

"The old creep asked me out first, you know," she continued. "He said he wanted to see me wearing something more feminine the next time he stopped in, said he'd love to buy me something 'pink—Candy pink,' he said. He said he wanted to see if my dragon was breathing fire and wanted to sooth the burn, then he said 'hot' like he was trying out for some bad porn show and I told him this, that he'd never in a million years see what my dragon is doing and that I don't wear *feminine* clothes that I know of and that I love the color brown and wear it much of the time—always have. I said, I love brown—sometimes with a pop of red or fuchsia or turquoise, but brown. Brown as dirt." We had all stopped eating by then and were staring at her in amazement. "He said that didn't sound like his décor but he'd make it work, that he loved brownies. I thought he was assuming I was a pothead which I am not by any stretch, a little here and there but not recently because I've been studying my ass off you know? But then I realized it might be racist, right? Or that he was making a joke about *Brownies* meaning the little Girl Scouts, and any or all of those things made him even creepier, right?"

"So what did you say?" we asked in unison.

"I said fuck you, I said I wear brown because I don't give a shit. I said I'd take a beret and some Thin Mint cookies over him any day." She looked at each of us and then slumped forward, young face cupped in her hands. "You all are so much better than that and it's really bad karma for that baby inside of you." She pointed at the pregnant belly among us. "And it really sucks for whoever out there does love you. You chicks are way too old for this; it's like high school and who the hell wants to go back to high school? That was terrible. He's a creepy old vampire, sucking your soul dry and then hanging you up in the closet like Bluebeard did all those poor girls. Did you ever read that one? Yikes, a good one but you want to be the smart girl who figures it all out before she gets murdered, right? Like let him be all fucked up by himself without pulling some poor idiot—no offense—down with him."

She showed us the pale underside of her right arm where it said: *To thine own self be true* and then right below in teeny tiny letters: *if you weren't invited to read this, you better get the hell back.*

"This guy I've been seeing loves reading me. He works at Costco on weekends and seems kind of lazy, but he's writing a novel and he votes and pays his taxes, so I'm giving him the benefit of the doubt. See? Another book. But he's smart and funny, says I'm his favorite bedtime read, and I say then he better not be plagiarizing. He cracked up over that. And speaking of cracks, that's where I put that one about how that's how the light gets in, but I'd get in trouble if I showed it here in the restaurant. But here's my very favorite, another one from Charlotte—I'd put the whole book if I could—and I'll try to show you without *cracking up*. Get it?" She laughed and turned, then raised her shirt up high enough that we could see her grandmother's chin and neck and below it in tiny script: *All these sights and sounds and smells will be yours to enjoy, _____ —this lovely world, these precious days . . .* "I think that's so beautiful," she said. "I left it blank where it's supposed to say *Wilbur* so anyone can enjoy it. The librarian read that book aloud and I never got over it. Every day she read a new chapter and she got so mad at the asshole boy in my class who kept trying to tell me the ending and ruin it all. I mean I knew what was coming. We all know something sad will happen, we just don't know what, right? Just that it will." She sighed, stood and pulled down her waistband and twisted to the side: *carpe the hell out of this diem.* "No rush but I can take your bill any time." She winked and then pulled the other side of her skirt down long enough for us to see half of a sketched-out spider web and what she called "words from the prophets." Bette Midler's *Fuck 'em if they can't take a joke* and Gilda Radner's *I base most of my fashion taste on what doesn't itch.* She turned, brogans squeaking, a living Bible of truth and common sense while we sat, feeling plain and cheap in our designer clothes, aware of how much time we had wasted talking about someone who had *never* been who we thought he was—*He* was the imaginary person—and we knew so little about each other, our present lives and jobs and interests. If we could go anywhere in the world, where would we go? And if we could conjure back to life one person, who would it be? And if we got a tattoo, what would it say about us? And what on earth would we do with this new wealth of time?

✳ Swinger

Marnie surveys the house and everything in it daily knowing this could be the last time she is here, the last time she fills the deep tub with bubbles so she doesn't notice the rust stains around the drain, or waters the overgrown azaleas out front. It could be the last time she sits in the porch swing and watches the convicts who regularly pick up trash along the interstate that runs just beyond the pasture where the neighbors have a few goats and cows, or the last time she settles into the too-soft mattress on Roland's bed wishing she could feel him there beside her. It is just a matter of time before they come to take everything and send her on her way. It isn't her house after all. She owns very little in this world, never has—an old Honda, her clothes, a couple of pieces of furniture, and a quilt she holds on to for sentimental reasons. Roland said that some day she would own half of this house, but that day never came to pass and now his daughter and wife will come and take whatever they think is of value and be done with him once and for all. They will take the will he never finished filling out and they will take the heavy safe box in his closet where he has a pistol and some old foreign money and all sorts of important papers.

They didn't even let her know where he was or what had happened until after they had already sent him off to the crematorium; two days later they pulled up in front of the house in a brand-new-looking car they never even turned off and left the heavy box containing all that was left of him on the stoop with a piece of yellow legal pad paper taped to the top. *Do with him as you please and vacate these premises as soon as possible.* She was there when they came and a part of her wanted to rush out onto the porch and scare them. She thought of taking Roland's gun and aiming it at them, but she had never held a gun in her life, so instead she picked up Roland's old Polaroid camera he used for work as an insurance adjuster—every day bringing home photos of what he referred to as *the crime scenes*: bent fenders and dog bites and faulty steps or wiring.

There were no accidents waiting to happen in their yard but the wife and daughter stopped and pointed at where she had used an old tire as a planter, filling it with pastel snapdragons and petunias. They shook their heads and laughed as if to say it looked stupid and then they pointed at the bumper sticker on her car that said I'M PRETTY SURE WHEN JESUS SAID LOVE YOUR ENEMY HE MEANT DON'T KILL HIM. Roland loved that bumper sticker and she reminded herself of that as the two women stood there shaking their heads. She snapped a picture when they were at their car and wouldn't see the curtains move or hear the whirr of the machinery as it spit out a cloudy square that slowly turned into their image. The daughter looked a lot like Roland, olive complexion and dark, wavy hair, a small muscular body like that of a gymnast. It looked better on a man but she was cute enough. The wife was long and bony-looking with a poof of yellow hair strategically brushed and sprayed to leave her looking like someone whose hair is naturally that way—wild and carefree; her dress was cut low to reveal her pale throat and cleavage where she still wore Roland's mother's tiny gold cross necklace.

That cross was something Roland had told Marnie about one of those nights they lay there in the dark and talked about any and everything that came to mind, like he asked about her name, saying how before her, he'd only heard it in a Hitchcock movie, which kind of creeped him out because that Marnie came out of nowhere and was frigid and a kleptomaniac.

"Well I didn't come from nowhere," she told him. "And I'm neither of those other things either."

"Well, I know you aren't frigid," he said, his broad hand heavy on her abdomen. "Found that out the day I met you." He laughed. "And nothing's missing that I can tell."

"I have never taken anything that wasn't mine," she told him. "In fact, I am so the other way that I always had a hard time voting for myself even if I wanted the job." She told how she was once nominated to be a student council representative and really wanted to win, people raising their hands with their eyes closed to vote, but she thought the other girl would probably be better at it and she didn't want people to see her with her hand raised for herself.

"Well that was just stupid," he told her. "If you don't go after what you want, who will do it for you?" The answer in the silence was *nobody. Nobody* will do it for you. She thinks of that often now. But then, she had laughed and turned the conversation to John the Baptist and how she always hated that picture where they have his bloody chopped-off head served up on a platter and found it hard to understand why somebody would want little children in the Sunday school room to see it and that was what made him think of his mother's gold cross necklace and what he called *the whole salvation thing*. He was a good storyteller and following his stories was like a history lesson or a scavenger hunt as she sought the various parts of his life she did not know. The cross was all he had left of his mother, and once, in the middle of a long, drawn-out fight with his wife, he had snatched the necklace from her throat, marched way down the road near that little churchyard at the edge of the pasture, and hurled it into the ditch where there was always debris and litter from passing cars, which was why the work crew was there so often. He had never given it to her to begin with. She had taken it—*stolen* it—from his special box where he kept a lot of things like a medal he got for going to Vietnam and another medal he got as a young boxer. "It didn't belong to her," he said. "She ruined it."

A nurse who lived down the road told Marnie that he was likely already dead when they brought him in to the emergency room. "If I'd been at work, I would've known to call you," the woman said apologetically. She was an older woman, plain in her lack of makeup or adornments of any kind, and she did not look at Marnie with an eye for judgment as so many people did. Perhaps it was because her own husband did not work at all and hadn't for years; perhaps she had her own fears of being judged, which kept her in a neutral place. "They called what they thought was his legal next of kin," she explained. "Everybody in town knew him." The woman touched her arm. "He was a really fine person."

Now she goes through the house touching the fabric of the drapes and the bedspread she picked out herself to surprise him. "It's blue," he'd said, which was true though that was not the answer she had hoped to get. She touches the mystery novel he'd been reading, turned facedown to hold his place. One night she opened it and read up to where he'd been, but it was scary so she watched an old sitcom instead, that nanny woman with the good hair and awful accent. He loved telling her the details of all those mysteries, always fascinated by how crimes are solved. He liked all those television shows, too, the ones that zoom in and show you cells and tissues and such like you might be in science class. She could take or leave that kind of show but what she did love was sitting there in the dark close to him and the way he always shielded her face with a pillow if something gory was coming. He told her their DNA was everywhere. His toenails snipped and flown off into the carpeting never to be seen again, which he took great pleasure in doing since his wife had always demanded he step outdoors to clip. He said that when Marnie sanded her rough, dry heels with that little sandpaper paddle the

DNA blew around in the air like little dust particles, that he had probably breathed and eaten her DNA. You are everywhere, he had said, and pointed to the hair in her hairbrush, or a single strand caught in a necklace or on the neck of her sweater or stuck to his own body after a good night.

His razor is still on the edge of the sink, an old-timey straight-edge razor like the one she first used shaving her legs, white thin strip up her shin proof of the danger. He had once run his finger up the scar lightly and told her how he wished he had known her then, that young girl with all of life ahead of her, but she is so glad he didn't know her then; she was a wandering accident looking for a place to happen. The toilet seat is up and she stares, trying to remember why that would be, since he has not been home since last Monday. Six days ago he left to go to the store. Her fingertips linger. He didn't always lift the seat to pee and sometimes he even sat. She teased him about it and he laughed. "I'm not lazy," he told her more than once. "But the doctor told me not to lift heavy objects."

There in the linen closet, at the back, under a stack of rags he used when washing the car, is a shoebox full of Polaroids. She found it almost three years ago, not long after they met and she moved in. What first got her attention was that it was his wife's old shoebox, a brand she had only seen in magazines and wasn't sure how to pronounce. The little picture on the side showed a strappy high heel and the label said it was peacock blue. But inside were photos. Most were "crime scenes," wrecked cars and burned houses and mug shots of dogs that bite, but there was also a manila envelope with others, nude shots, twenty-three of them in fact—all different people. His wife was in there, she recognized a much younger version of her, and she recognized other people she had seen in town from time to time, that woman who runs the dance school and always runs around town in tights and leotards, and the woman who is married to the mayor, who knows if she was then or not. Marnie didn't *know* any of these people; she grew up two towns over and likely would have passed on through this town except she met him and he asked her to stay awhile. She'd closed the box back, suddenly feeling like a thief, and placed it back just as it was.

He had several times referred to his "swinger years" and the long list of women who preceded her, many before he ever got married, a couple during but only there at the end when it got really bad, quite a few after he moved out and into this house. He had grown up in this house and then rented it after his mother died. He said it was a good thing he had held on to it. *No place like home*, he said. He had told her that his wife had allowed her family down in Georgia to assume they were still living together as man and wife, that for her the lie and appearance was more important than anything else and he decided just to wait her out, figured someday she'd actually want a divorce and a life.

"And don't you want a divorce and a life?" she asked.

"Sure, sure I do," he said, but that was in the very beginning and so she didn't ask anymore.

"Where do I fit in?" she asked one night, but he was already sleeping, the moonlight catching the face of the much younger man, the person who had teased and asked all those women to strike a pose. The next time he asked her to tell him something about herself, she almost said no one had ever asked to take a picture of her naked, but instead she said she was a really good student in school, which she thought might surprise him given she had always worked entry-level retail and waitress jobs. They said she was a girl with potential and when they made groups based on IQ she was always out of place, separated from *her* group—the kids most likely *not* to go to college—and eventually she decided to quit trying so as not to be taken out of her comfort zone. She saw herself similar to those goats out in the pasture, wide blank eyes. When one got lost it freaked out; even when the grass was better, it suffered to be away from the warm comfort of its own kind.

Now she longs for the warmth she has depended on and gotten used to. A lot can happen in three years. You can get pregnant and see your baby turn two. You can put in an asparagus patch and have it ready for harvest or a vine that leaps after sleeping and creeping. Wine and cheese can age and bones can heal. You can do most of high school, move from one leap year to the next. You can look back and feel relieved by the distance like miles and miles in your rearview mirror. It is a long time when you string together all the nights and hours of it.

In all the pictures, the women are holding on to the poster of his bed, the very one right there. The closet door is standing open and she goes over to push it closed. The women all posed with the window behind them, the very window she is standing in front of, the window that is not on his side of the bed but hers—*her* window. She had long thought that it was only a matter of time before he asked to shoot her, and she had often practiced exactly how she was going to pose when her turn came. The photos made her feel bad, like he had a big secret he kept from her even though they talked in the dark in a way that seemed everything got said. One night she even brought up that old camera the Swinger, saying how for some reason the little jingle got all stuck in her head. "It's Polaroid's camera, it's almost alive, it's only nineteen dollars and ninety-five." He joined in: "Swing it up—yeah yeah—it says yes. . . ." He said he hadn't thought of that in years and what about those Benson and Hedges commercials when the cigarettes kept getting stuck like in elevator doors. All the cigarette ads for that matter, and then he did the music for Marlboro country. "Hey and what about 'I'd rather fight than switch!'" She tried to keep it on the camera and how it told you what to do, when it was a perfect time to take the shot. "Wouldn't it be nice to be told the right answer?" she asked. Like the Magic 8 Ball. "Wouldn't it be nice to have a swinger for life?"

"You do," he said.

"Are you a swinger?"

"Used to be."

"I wish I had the answer. Should I stay or go? Like I wish I had a GPS implanted in my head saying things like 'Recalculate!' 'Don't go there!' 'Make a U-turn.'"

"How about stay?" he asked and pulled her close. He had a tattoo he got years ago—barbed wire around his bicep.

"Is this to keep people out?" she had asked.

"All except you," he said, "it's to keep you in," and once again she chose the comfort in the moment over an interruption. *To keep you.* The memory of him saying that stays there like a bright patch of life where she was so aware of her happiness even as she was sitting smack in the middle of it. She had had another patch like that, but she had to go all the way back into childhood to find it—her great aunt and uncle, a shade tree, the ping of peas being shelled into a large tin colander, the smell of hard work and rusty well water, sweet fermenting peaches by the big enamel sink and a yard full of papershell pecans in the fall. That was a bright patch and she had wanted to stay there forever, too.

Still, knowing that shoebox was there haunted her and made her feel left out, but what else was new? She was one of those women people didn't give things to and never had. Not flowers or jewelry or love poems. She was the kind of invisible woman who might be referred to as sturdy or dependable, smart and practical. Roland had even called her his rock, which is what she felt she had been for a series of different men in her life; it seemed they all sowed their oats and dabbled in romance and then settled with the big hard rock; they could climb under it or use it to mark their cave. And she tried her best to roll into it. After all, what did she really deserve? She came late into a clean, clear sense of what she wanted in life, and oddly, what she had found here with Roland has been it—home—a dream come true—and everything in place and hung out to dry except that box and his getting divorced, which she had begun to trust would one day come.

Once, when she asked again, where she fit in, he called her his caboose—the last car in a long line—*no one can ever come after you*, he said and hugged her backside. She was aware then more than ever before how she had the kind of body that should have had children but it was not meant to be. *No one can ever come after you.* And now that was true. His death had guaranteed that. "But they can make me leave," she tells him, whispering the words as she runs her hands across the back of his chair. She would swear she heard him sigh, heard him sniff, heard the creak of the floor behind her.

She wanders back out onto the porch to watch the highway crew. Often they are out there, picking up trash and weeding, down in the ditch where Roland had gone to discard his mother's necklace and who knows what else? His wife had found it. He said she spent hours searching so she could walk back in twirling it around her finger, nearly hitting him in the eye with it, and saying wouldn't it be a shame if people knew he had broken and trashed the one thing his mother had treasured. The one thing she had asked him to keep and hold close to his heart.

My heart, he told Marnie, his voice catching, and she was relieved they had already turned out the light. *It was my heart.*

The men arrive in what looks like an old school bus now cheaply painted a pale sick yellow with the words INMATES WORKING CREW stenciled on the side. Steel mesh covers the windows and all the men wear orange vests. Sometimes they turn and look at her; on occasion one has lifted his hand in a wave until jerked back to attention by one of the men with a rifle at either end of the line. These men stand with their feet apart and their guns held out front, ready at a moment's notice. One day she returned an inmate's wave. She felt ashamed not to, somehow ashamed that she was watching them, and then she also felt ashamed for the officers in charge to see her being friendly to a criminal. If they were without their guns, those men would disperse like buckshot, arms and legs pumping down the ditch and across the pasture and churchyard, or in the other direction to the interstate and on into the woods beyond. It might be that some of them had already gotten used to the small life of prison—the bad but filling dinners, the comfort of one's own cot. Right after Vietnam, Roland had worked briefly in the prison system. He said they'd hired him for his muscles and his tattoos and because he knew how to throw a punch that nine out of ten times would knock somebody's lights out.

A punching bag hangs from the front porch and now she goes and wraps her arm around it and pulls it close, breathes in the sunbaked dustiness of the old leather. Every day Roland would come out and move around, punching and dancing; his gloves reminded her of enormous eggplants and she loved the heavy, rhythmic thuds of his punches and the squeaks and whines of the flooring as he moved. He was in his fifties, ten years older than her, but it would be hard to guess that. His muscles were tight and he kept himself lean, no paunch or love handles. The only thing that might've revealed his age was the papery texture of his skin, thinner and looser than a young man's skin; it made her think of those old papershell pecans in her aunt and uncle's yard. Penny a pecan, her aunt once paid her. *Penny for your thoughts*, people sometimes say, though she had never felt anyone honestly cared before Roland. Those pecans cracked so easily, not like the tough hardshelled ones in the yard of the people she stayed with after her aunt died. *They'll stain your fingers*, children were always warned, but everything good did, it seemed. Pecans and pomegranates, peaches and blackberries, those magic markers that smelled so good at school.

They will likely take the television, still tuned to the Weather Channel where he always kept it for a quick forecast during the day. Even if she turns it to watch something at night, she always puts it back where he liked to keep it. Sometimes, she leaves it on, turned low as she stretches out in bed and tries to sleep. Sometimes she can convince herself that he is right in there listening and that very soon she will hear the creak and feel the slope of the bed, smell the scent of him as he moves in close and reaches for her.

She has seen pictures of Roland when his young tanned skin stretched tight on his flesh: a high school football star, a young father, a young Marine on his way to Vietnam, and once she even felt guilty that in her mind she was making love to the man her own age with his dark thick hair and broad muscular chest. In her mind, his duffle bag was in the corner of the room—just home from the service and starved for only her. There is no wife and there is no daughter in this picture. She is not the caboose but the engine. She is a star, the first and most important part.

He really was a star in this town, someone everybody knew, and he walked like somebody who had been a star, arms slightly lifted but held out from his sides. He was solid and strong. When she first met him she could tell he had been and still was a prize. That's how he introduced himself to her at Jiffy Lube. He just right out told her that he was a star in this town and he laughed.

She thought how he reminded her of a creature she had seen in a book at school years before, half-man and half-horse, legs and chest as stocky as a Shetland pony. *Centaur.* She looked it up and rubbed her fingertip around the lines of the image. Part man and part myth. He has always seemed that way to her.

And he did love her; he did. He would have married her in a second if he'd ever gotten divorced. She wanted to ask why didn't he then? Why didn't he get a divorce? She wanted to say that if he didn't, she would have to leave, and maybe that was why she had waited, not wanting to have to make good on such a statement if it came to that. Still, she had promised herself to at least *ask* all the questions. But she didn't get the chance. Like so many things in life, she didn't get the chance and now she has to just let it go. She hears a sound in the living room, probably the cat, but her first thought is that it's him, leaning forward in his chair to lace his sneakers so he can come out here and box in the late afternoon light that makes everything look so much better than it is, like the whole world has been airbrushed. Even the convicts start to look soft and muted, their bending and picking graceful as if in slow motion.

That old yellow bus is parked right near the churchyard, waiting for late in the day when all those men—who knows what they did to get there?—will file back on, taking the same seats that were once filled with children whose worries might have been about undone homework or not wearing the right brand of clothes. If they reached their hands deep into the creases of those cracked vinyl seats, there's no telling what they might find, so many clues to so many lives, so much DNA. People are getting released right and left because of DNA, people who have been forced into lives and punishment that didn't belong to them. How do they keep from hating, or do they? What do they do with resentment and anger? She could reach your hand deep into the cool of a seat and find a pencil once used and chewed on by some kid on the bus on an average day with weather like today. Once upon a time a single individual with a whole life up ahead sat there. Clues are good. Clues are important. But they are no substitute for a warm body; they are no substitute for a voice in the darkness.

The prison guard closest to her stands, lazily leaning on a fence rail with his gun held across his chest. The other one is at the other end, pacing back and forth from the ditch to the pasture and back. And all those men just look hot and tired in those orange vests. They look old from this distance, bending and stooping, sweat pouring and hearts pounding—and what are they thinking? Are they thinking of home or how they might break off and run? And what was Roland thinking? He was in someone's driveway under the hot midday sun. He was getting the facts about someone who was going door-to-door selling aerial photographs from another time. You could see how your house or land looked a hundred years ago. Only when the man got to this house, a little orphaned terrier mutt had come rushing out from under the steps and tore into the man's ankle. When Roland arrived to take the picture, the little dog wagged its tail and flipped onto its back like it had never hurt a flea. She heard all this from the owner of the dog when she went to get Roland's car and try to put together his last day. She had a spare key and no one else had bothered to come get it. She wanted to sit where he had sat. She wanted to slide down onto the ground and see what he saw. There was a hedge of abelia, the little white blossoms filled with bees in the glaring sun, and there was a green-and-white webbed yard chair leaned against the carport wall where a child had written his name in chalk—*Max*—a pair of jumper cables hanging close by. There was nothing extraordinary for him to see, hard-baked dirt and an unkempt porch, and that alone made her feel so sad and needing to roll his day back to their waking, the sky just turning light in the window on her side.

The man told her that it all happened so fast—Roland went pale and asked the man for a glass of water and when he came back out, Roland was slumped in the passenger seat of his old Honda. He never said anything else. For her, the last word was *later*. Usually he said, "Later gator." But that day he ended on later. He said he was off to the crime scene, yet another angry terrier bites annoying trespasser. He said, "It's hard for a terrier to forgive those trespasses," and he laughed. He said, "Later."

The wife and daughter will come and expect her to be gone or they will ask her to leave. Then they will root through all of his things and likely throw most everything away. They will find that box of Polaroids and the wife will root through and steal her own before she proclaims him trash and worthless. They will say that's just like him and Thank God they have been spared living with him all these years.

Why did you leave me out? She asks out loud. And why did you leave me here alone to tend to all this? There is silence and then she thinks she hears a sigh.

* * *

By the time the bus is loaded, the sun is disappearing, and she dreads stepping back indoors and turning on a light. She dreads having to face the looks of his wife and daughter, the judgment and ridicule they will bring. They will point and laugh at her just as they had her garden. But they don't know her. They don't know a thing about her. What did any of it matter? "Why did you leave me alone?" she whispers again, opening the door to see him there, only as soon as her eyes see him, her brain has sent the message that no, this is not him.

The man in the shadows is much taller than Roland. When her eyes adjust she can make out his features better: burnt copper arms with a big tattoo of a purplish rose with a knife through it. He's a white guy baked in the sun too long and he hasn't aged well at all, deep ruddy creases in his neck and forehead, hair bleached like straw. He has Roland's pistol, the foreign money on the floor behind him.

"Can I help you?" she asks.

"Maybe."

Her heart is pounding. "That's my husband's gun," she says. "If you're wanting to buy or borrow it you'll need to come back when he's here."

"Your husband?" he looks at her hand, where there is no ring.

"Yes."

"What's his name?"

"Roland."

"I believe I just saw Roland. I believe he's in a box in yonder on your dresser." He laughs. "Barely cool, too. My sympathies for your loss." He says he may look like somebody that don't read the paper, but he does and he knows Roland died. "I used to rent from Roland, right here in this house. Me and my wife lived here."

"So what do you want?"

"Car keys," he says. "And for you to shut up."

"I'm not scared," she said to herself.

"You would be if you saw what I left behind me."

"Are you with the prison bus?"

He laughs. "No, and I'm doing my goddamn best to avoid it."

"Are you gonna kill me?"

"I don't know," he says. "Who would even know or care if I did?"

She thinks how those are two very different questions. It might take awhile unless the wife and daughter show up as they have threatened to do. The cat would certainly notice and care. She'd be hungry. And the work crew, they'd notice. They'd say what's become of that gal that watches us at the end of the day? They might see a buzzard circling, might notice there are still sheets on the line and a collection of newspapers on the walk. She pictures herself dead and waiting and the stark, harsh view of that snaps her back. "The convicts would notice. And my coworkers."

"That could be," he says. "But there's a lot of time in there ain't it?"

She thinks of that woman in Georgia who read aloud to somebody threatening to kill her and it saved her life and she got on the news, but all Marnie sees is the *TV Guide* and that murder mystery of Roland's, which is probably not a good idea.

"What do you like to read?" she asks. "You know, to relax."

"Do you want to die or something?"

"I don't really care," Marnie says. "Almost did it myself once. In fact I was on my way to do it for real when I met Roland and then everything turned around. You can *not* love your life but still love life, the idea of it, and I'm one of those stupid people who wakes up every day thinking today's your big day, girl. Today it all gets better. But if you knew for sure you were going to kill me, then I'd likely go mix myself a drink that would put an elephant in a coma. I quit when I met Roland—he was my drug of choice—but that's what I'd do for sure." She knows she is talking too much, but it's been so long it feels good to shape all the words, good to exert all the breath that goes with them.

"You know," the man says, "when I did time they called me Hulk Hogan because of my hair and I liked that I scared people. It's good to scare people. So first night, I grab me this young Black guy and I took him to the bathroom. I said say a goddamned word out there and I'll kill you, and every night I'd haul his little skinny ass in there and I'd slam my hand against the wall, see, like forceful slams and I'd end with a real slap to his face to bring tears to his eyes. And nobody bothered either of us, see?"

She wants to say that was nice of him but decides to stay silent. He keeps slapping the pistol against his thigh as he stands sideways so he can see her and the field out front.

"You know sometimes things start happening and you can't help it," he says. "And then it's out of your control. All out of your control."

She nods.

"Sometimes you do or don't do things even when you know you should. Jesus." He shakes his head as if to remove something from his mind then turns back. "You're mighty calm for a woman in this situation. I suspect my wife would be screaming her head off or maybe crouched over in the corner crying. I suspect that's it. Crouched in the corner screaming, begging. I can hear her right now—'Let me explain, let me explain.'" He grits his teeth and shakes his head like a dog that's latched on to something.

"I've lost what I care about," she says.

"Me, too, lady, me too!" He slaps his chest and then moves the hair back from his face with the nose of the pistol. "Look, I'm not a killer, okay? Or I wasn't. I never set out to do it." He points to the photo of Roland as a young man in his boxing trunks. "So what killed him?"

"His heart."

"You been with him long?"

"Three years," and she tells him all she can think to say about Roland while he watches the sun going down. How he was a man who rarely liked to go anywhere but when he did, like to hear music or to see something on a stage, he got the seats with armrests, that kind of ticket. And he had a real good vocabulary and he was proud of that, like he would use a word like *copacetic* like that was nothing. Or he might look at the color of the man's skin and describe it like burnished brandy. She heard him say that once about the skin of a beautiful woman they bought some melons from at a roadside market along the highway. *Burnished Brandy.*

* * *

When the prison bus has pulled away and the sun is just a sliver of orange over the field, she goes and finds the spare key to Roland's car. "Whether you kill me or not, I do have one favor to ask." She holds the key out in front of her and backs into the bedroom.

"Aw come on now. Isn't it enough I listened to all this shit?"

"Please," she hands him the camera. "Just take my picture." She turns on the harsh overhead light and then quickly undresses, leaving her clothes in a heap on the floor, the key on top of them, and goes to stand where all the others had stood. He eyes the key and then her body but now, with the camera up near his eye, she pretends he is Roland and she leans into the post, cool wood brushing her hip, as she acts out the scene she has practiced so many times; she tilts her head, she licks her lips. Her heart pounds with the thought that someone could be here any minute—the wife and daughter, the policemen on his trail. She breathes in and arches her neck, breasts pushed forward, toe pointed out like a dancer and she looks right at him and then beyond, where the yard will soon be dark, a black, moonless night. There is a click and a whirr and when she opens her eyes, it's to the sound of him slamming the door, Roland's car cranked and then gone. The square on the edge of the dresser is a blur—bedpost, window frame, the slow recognition of her own skin and hair. She has the thought that she should have asked him to take another. She could have been the only girl in the box with two.

✳ A Simple Question

There was something in the late winter light that tugged Anna's mind to that day and she wasn't sure why. Over twenty-five years had passed and yet there it was—a gray winter afternoon and a long-ago friend. They were in the parking lot across from the theater, the Colonial—she remembers that part clearly—and she had to walk carefully to avoid lingering patches of ice. She wasn't wearing her boots, having opted to risk the good shoes, but then was sorry not to have the security of hard rubber traction. It was a Sunday in late February and the whole day had felt like dusk. The show crowd had thinned and the last of the cars were filing from the lot. They had gone to see *Death of a Salesman*, the matinee, and while walking around before the show, had actually seen Hal Holbrook sitting in a restaurant. Was it really him? they wondered. How could he eat? They stared too long, because he smiled and raised his hand. She will never forget that, the image returning so clearly with the recent news of his death. But that day, in the city with Muriel, their words and laughter muffled by scarves and coat collars, it had made her recount having seen a striking man on Boylston Street years before—an elegant camel hair coat and trimmed moustache. She told Muriel she knew it was either Walter Cronkite or Captain Kangaroo and after a stunned pause had let out a loud, involuntary "Walter Cronkite!" He turned, smiled, and waved and she was so relieved she hadn't screamed "Captain Kangaroo!" They laughed and then Muriel said she had something she wanted to ask—how had she said it? *I want to ask you something* or *I have a question.* Then she said that perhaps it would be better to wait until they were seated, or after the show, better without all the distractions. She said this when Anna stopped to study the menu of a restaurant, suggesting they eat there some time, perhaps the next time they met for a show.

At the time, Anna was thinking a lot about her apartment, a small one-bedroom, fourth-floor walkup. She was thrilled not to have a roommate but also missed having someone to share her life, someone that is, other than Muriel, who people might very well have thought was her mother. Muriel got divorced later that year so it could have been something about that, maybe she'd known it was coming and wanted to run her thoughts by someone else. And she often talked about her son, who had left college in the middle of his freshman year and moved back home—so there was another possibility.

Anna had thought often what unlikely friends they were—
Muriel was twice her age—and yet, they had a lot of common
interests and taught at the same junior high school, both in language arts. They both loved walking around the city, going to the
theater and museums, and they both disliked their principal, a
man who stood too close and explained everything in exaggerated
enunciation as if talking to a toddler or dog. *Or imbecile*, Muriel
once added. Anna was barely twenty-five when she took that job
and had known no one, so she had welcomed seeing Muriel each
day, the wry glances at meetings and laughter at lunch.

It had been only natural that they began to get together outside of school. In those early years, Muriel was encouraging in
all ways, telling Anna she would have a host of friends in no
time, that she was a stellar teacher, that she imagined Anna
would soon have all kinds of dates, and then who knew where
life would take her. *Enjoy this window*, Muriel had said and
laughed. *You won't believe how quickly things can change.*
Muriel seemed old at the time, a husband and a child in the
seventh grade, a house in the suburbs; she often brought baked
goods—bread or cakes—for the break room at school. That was
in the very beginning and Anna relied on her maternal good-
ness, the care and hopeful future projections of what Anna's life
might bring. They laughed over Anna's domestic mishaps—the
time she purchased MSG for a recipe, the fact that she didn't
know a dryer filter had to be cleaned or that you shouldn't put
grease down the sink. Back then, when they met, Muriel had
said that she was the happiest she had ever been and felt closer
to her husband than she ever dreamed possible. Their son had
some challenges in school, but he was about to turn thirteen and

doing so much better. They had hired a tutor; they were hopeful. Such a relief for him to have a friend, she had said.

Anna wasn't domestic at all in those years, but she loved everything about her tiny apartment except the pigeons roosting on the windowsill and the squirrels living in the walls. At night she could hear them, acorns rolling, nails scratching, even though the landlord had assured her that he had it all under control. He said he really doubted they would find a way into the apartment. He said it had only happened once in the thirty years he'd been there; he could set a trap, and would if it got worse, but that really is a horrible sound, he said, not to mention that they'd all be smelling it. *It's a quandary*, he kept saying. *And remember—squirrels are not rats and it's almost spring.*

It was a breezy February day. Valentine hearts and cardboard cupids decorated the window of a stationery shop from the week before and she recalled Muriel commenting about the groundhog having seen his shadow—more cold coming. She doesn't remember telling Muriel about the squirrels in the wall and the way she could hear them scratching right near her bed, but she must have, especially with the mention of another rodent.

She recalled how she had envied those like Muriel with so much of life fixed and decided in their suburban backyards, garage doors that magically opened to a kitchen the size of her whole apartment, a life partner, a child, a pet. She was only at Muriel's home a few times, the son's bar mitzvah her first, and she was only invited because she mentioned in the teacher's lounge that a friend had broken a date and she had nothing to do. Muriel even arranged a ride for her with another teacher in their school. Anna remembered how Muriel's husband had raised a glass and said, *Today you are a man and tomorrow you go back to seventh grade!* Muriel and her husband stood together that day, arms entwined, their son out on the dance floor laughing with a new confidence from this moment of popularity. Another time, Anna was shopping out that way and stopped by to return a book Muriel had loaned her and was invited in at what seemed a stressful time; there was an uncomfortable pause when she found the three of them in the kitchen, sitcom laughter in some distant room. The son was in high school by then, applying to schools, smoking a lot of pot. Muriel said that every time she tried to talk to him, to understand what was going on in his life he said: *You want to know what's wrong with me? How about what the fuck is wrong with you?*

The question Anna recalls vividly was the one he asked at his party when he was thirteen and reading aloud from a book of riddles he'd received as a gift. The spotlight was on him and it was clear that his parents were enjoying his getting attention as much as he was. There were all the silly riddles of course— hands and legs/clocks and chairs—but the one Anna recalls was: "What is the question you can ask anywhere in the world, get different answers each time and yet always be correct?" She could see him there, hair cowlicked, crust of chocolate cake on the edge of his mouth. He was an awkward kid who came into the room and everything was instantly topsy-turvy, lamp shades crooked and rugs flipped up; it seemed he was always on the verge of nervous laughter because he had a secret or knew something you didn't.

In high school, there were suspensions and drugs. He told his mother that he wished he was dead, and then later that he wished *she* was dead. Muriel had told Anna about this while they were walking Beacon Hill on the third Thursday in May—a day devoted to the annual garden tour, when they made their way along the uneven brick sidewalks to peer into tiny, often sunless spaces transformed into paradise: brickwork in elaborate patterns, mirrors and fountains and statues. They read aloud the descriptions in the program, the various plant names like incantations that might open the wrought iron gates and heavy, ancient doors that led to other lives: trumpet vine and bleeding hearts, astilbe, pulmonaria, laurel, lilac, euonymus. *What can a mother say to that?* she asked. *God.*

Another day, they made up their own tour based on Muriel's idea—apartments of long-dead writers. Three on Pinckney Street alone: Alcott and Thoreau and Hawthorne. Plath on Willow and Frost on Mt. Vernon. Muriel's idea was that they should read something at each stop, and she had books in her tote with pages carefully marked. They had stood at the foot of Pinckney Street, the river at their backs, before climbing up the hill, and it was there Muriel had pointed to a third-floor bay where she had once lived with two other young teachers, a view of the river and a preschool across the street where at recess kids, all bundled in snowsuits, held on to a long rope with a teacher on each end; if a child started to slip on the icy bricks, they yanked the rope and popped them right back up.

"I wish you could have known my son when he was a toddler," she had said and smiled, but it was hard to pull together the image of a windblown, bundled cherub with the awkward, riddle-telling boy, and especially not with that of the angry young man who wished her dead. "When I was your age and up in that window," she paused, then shook her head as if to dispel whatever words were coming next and reached for one of her many quotes selected for the day: Plath's ". . . numb as a fossil. Tell me I'm here" to Alcott's "I hate ordinary people!" She never let the somber tone last too long, always looking for something that might bring a smile, and perhaps that was what was different on that February day. The lifts were getting harder and harder to find.

And for Anna, it was getting harder and harder to listen to the sadness and the denial in her voice, the blame of the boy's father, his teachers. It was hard to respond to the regret and grief, that episode his freshman year; everything seemed okay and then. *And then.* How many times had Muriel told that story? He drained his bank account and got out on the highway. They had no idea where he was, and it was days before he called from a motel in Tucson without any money. Her husband had called her an enabler, said he couldn't take it, and then got a divorce, a new wife, a new life, but that was all later of course, and information Anna only heard second hand from another teacher in the school who lived in the same town. That day at the theater, Muriel had checked her phone often, a weak smile if she saw Anna notice.

But what was the question? *There's something I want to ask you,* she had said. Did she wait for intermission, or did they never circle back? They had great seats, Hal Holbrook completely transformed into Willy Loman, and afterward, when they stood in the parking lot and talked about the play—how Linda Loman said: "he's only a little boat looking for a harbor."

They marveled at the power of those words and the effect of staring at the set—the house where they had lived and struggled—*lived*—while also seeing what was not on stage, the distant crash of Willy's car wrapped around a tree, the shocking end of it all, and what about those haunting last words?: "We're free." A mortgage all paid. Something completed, and yet. *And yet.* Anna will remember that for the rest of her life, that February day, the sharp smell of the river ready to thaw, exhaust from the turnpike trapped in the low ceiling of gray. *We're free.*

At some point in one of the many conversations along the way, Anna had voiced horror that Muriel's husband kept a gun locked in his closet; she'd told Muriel she would *never* live with a gun in the house and that it was absolutely clear her son needed treatment, perhaps serious medication, or tough love, as she'd read about recently and seen on television, Oprah or Jane Pauley, someone talking in the background while she straightened her apartment for another day and looked forward to going out with friends her own age. Finally, friends her own age, too many friends it seemed, and a relationship that would carry her into the future and her *real* life. "I bet once he gets straightened out, his dad will want to return and then you'll have a decision," she had told Muriel. "That will be a big decision, won't it? Whether or not you let him come back. And what about some day when your son gets married? You can tell all these stories to his fiancée and everyone will laugh." Now, she shudders with the memory.

Muriel smiled, or what at the time seemed a smile, as if to say, oh yes, how smart, you are so right. As if suddenly, the light blared through and she realized something she hadn't seen before and yet, now isn't it obvious that what she was really thinking was *Oh my dear ignorant friend, you know nothing. Wait until you have children; wait until the person you have vowed to share through thick and thin can't take it anymore. Just you wait.* But she also was above saying such a thing. The words *just you wait* would not have occurred to someone like Muriel.

What time is it? That was the answer to that long-ago riddle, the universal question that yields different answers but all correct. A thirteen-year-old boy stands in the spotlight, his five minutes of glory, proud parents with their arms entwined, kids from school gathered around him, new suit, shiny belt and shoes, a tie purchased just for the occasion. His party, his celebration, his step into manhood. On that day, he had friends and proud parents and the gift of not knowing all that lay ahead of him.

And here she is, years and miles from that day in a town not unlike Muriel's where children wait in front of the house for the school bus to arrive. A place where the local news reports are the kind that get laughed at by the rest of the world: someone dumped trash in the recycling bin at the grocery store; a squirrel was in a tree acting strange; heads of cabbage were tossed around and left on the school ground. *Why?*

Now, standing at the sink, making the bed, staring out the window, grading papers, the thought of all the words not spoken seizes her. *Dear Muriel*, she thinks. *Dear Muriel*, and she thinks how sometimes the Universe gives an answer before we understand the question. There in the dark theater, there at the end, they sat in silence. The scene plays and even knowing what is coming, they are shocked by the crash, shocked by the humbling sense of loss and the awareness of how vulnerable each life. Muriel has been dead for several years now, her son as well, and yet each time Anna remembers, there is shock. By the time she heard about Muriel's illness, Anna was at a different school, and it was only by chance she ran into an old colleague who mentioned it—Muriel's years with her son and the sad choice he made, then her own health issues she kept to herself. This question comes to Anna: if she went to the city and walked those same steps, would she see something? Hal Holbrook in a restaurant? DEATH OF A SALESMAN on the marquee? Willy Loman resurrected and once again filled with hopeful promises? Would she see her young single self step from her dark apartment and hurry along the city streets to see Muriel waiting there on the corner with a big smile, hands deep in the pockets of her down coat?

They sat that day, elbows touching, not a sound to be heard in the theater as their minds fixed on the imagined accident in the distance, the same way her mind now can't think of Muriel's old house without seeing her son, hanging there in the mudroom where a Little Tikes tractor had grown invisible over the years. But that day, after the curtain call, after the lights came up, they walked outside where it was almost dark and lingered in the parking lot. It was their last outing. Anna is almost sure of that now, and what did she even do in her apartment that she rushed back to that day? She was eager to get home, hands in pockets and head bent to the cold, an urgency in her steps as she walked the many blocks. Did she stop in Blockbuster for a rental? DeLuca's for something she couldn't afford to eat? Did she call her still-living parents or wait until the next day to avoid the slow blue Sundays that plagued her for much of her young life? Did she watch something mindless on television? Knit? Grade papers? Did she even wonder what it was Muriel had wanted to ask, or was she distracted by the fact that there were squirrels in the walls and a pigeon roosting on her bedroom windowsill that overlooked an alley and dumpster, and she had boxes to pack, a move up ahead; she was moving into her life. It was a dark Sunday in February when she had no husband, no children, no mortgage. Her parents were alive and far away, healthy enough that she could complain about her conversations with them and not worry for a minute. She hadn't known what it felt like for a parent to die or for a marriage to feel threatened, for a child to lash out in anger; she hadn't known how sometimes you just need someone to listen. That day she had walked quickly, protecting shoes she tossed out twenty years ago, then climbed the four flights of stairs to her dark, tiny space where an old radiator whined and some creature with no sense of time clawed at the walls to get free.

✳ Baby in the Pan

Nobody cares about the little baby in a pan that Theresa has been looking at over and over on the computer, a little bloody bird-looking thing. A woman from her church sent it to her last week, and she had not been able to stop looking. This was the same woman—Faye Pitman—who organized the community flea market to raise money for the needy. *And I mean the real needy*, she liked to say, *not those just looking for an easy handout.* Faye Pitman was a leader and the kind of person that Theresa had always feared as much as she admired. Only a confident person could wear those big gold epaulettes and matching belt buckle that Faye wore at a recent meet and greet event. Theresa liked to be included and noticed by Faye—Faye loved Theresa's cheese biscuits made with Rice Krispies and a dash of cayenne pepper, for instance—but she did *not* like to be singled out for questions like when Faye quizzed her about her daughter, Candy, who had a baby without a man in sight and has a tattoo of a dragon that wraps all around her leg. "At least," Faye wrote when she sent the video, "that grandson of yours didn't end up like this!"

"Who in the hell is that woman?" Candy, who recently said she wants to be called Zandy—"short for something sophisticated like Alexandra"—said, "and why would she send you such an awful message?"

"She's just relieved you let little Dillon live," Theresa said, "and so am I, even though you have no earthly idea who the daddy is."

"Of course, I know who the daddy is. I chose him." Candy/Zandy said and then she said that she is tired of all the *propaganda* from people like "that idiot Faye woman." She said, if that was a *real* photo of a *real* baby, it was a rare sight compared to all the unwanted children on the planet and all the poor young women who died trying *not* to have a baby. "How about I send you and Faye some footage of starving children or those sexually abused in their own beds?" Candy had all kinds of information she was ready to give like she might've been Moses come down from the mountaintop; she said the occurrence of such a late-term abortion (that's what she called that poor baby in the pan) was a rare thing and who knew what the sad circumstances might be. She said it was more likely someone's sad miscarriage. She talked cells and clusters and what-have-you until Theresa wanted to throw a pan *at* her and she could have because Candy was standing right there in the kitchen in those short shorts she's too old to be wearing with that scaly green dragon looking like he's breathing fire on her you know what. Theresa was sorry she ever even showed her what Faye sent, but she was always hoping they might connect on something that would make Candy into a believer and then, thank God, people like Faye would stop judging Theresa for something completely out of her control.

Candy starts talking and can't stop, like she's talking to one of her students, and Theresa gets tired of listening. Give somebody a classroom and they think they can preach and teach the whole population. Candy teaches physical education, which Theresa thinks is like saying she teaches playtime. Oscar had said, "I paid all that money for you to teach recess? Hell girl. Who doesn't know recess?" Candy had thought it was fine and laughed when Oscar said things like that, Daddy's girl through and through, but don't let Theresa say the sky is blue or the grass is green. And Candy/Zandy also walks in and thinks she can touch all of Theresa's collection of dolls without asking, too, even though Theresa has told her a million times not to do that and not to go sifting through all her Ashton Drake and Franklin Mint certificates of authenticity.

"Franklin Graham is speaking over in Raleigh," Theresa said, the word *Franklin* stuck in her head and knowing exactly what she was doing but it was like she couldn't stop herself and Candy had started it all by saying that that baby wasn't even a real baby but something Faye might've made up, Faye who cared about the needy, the real needy, and who bought high end lingerie in Southern Pines and had even shown Theresa the receipt when Theresa had felt the silk and marveled that those things must've cost a small fortune.

"So?"

"What do you mean so?"

"I mean so what? Just another failed son trying to ride his daddy's coattail and I wasn't even that impressed with the daddy."

"What?" Theresa turned with her hand raised wanting to hit or throw something. "How dare you say such a thing. I'm surprised lightning doesn't strike that hard head of yours for being so sacrilegious."

"Oh, come on." Candy turned and stuck that green scaly leg out and tapped her big sneaker like she might've been playing the Hokey Pokey. "I'm sure he did some good things but all I ever heard people talk about was how handsome they thought he was."

"He couldn't help being handsome."

"Well, I didn't even think he was," she said and laughed great big. "Not my type. Daddy and I always thought it was funny you and all those women had a crush on him."

"How can you say that?"

"It's true."

"It's not true, and who knows what your type is other than invisible?"

"It's *true* that that is what I think and it's true that Daddy thought it was funny and you have no idea what my type is. There's a whole billboard of Billy Graham on the highway up around Asheville and if you will recall, I used to live there and drove by it all the time, so I have plenty of experience to base my opinion. I think Daddy was much better looking but I guess he wasn't *godly* enough for you."

Theresa ignored that last part; it gave her an aching stab to have Oscar's face conjured so easily right there in the kitchen, those liquid brown eyes like Dr. Zhivago and that lopsided smile, always a little bashful as a result of growing up with so little, or so he said. He liked to tell that joke she hated about how they were so poor, his mama had to cut holes in his pockets so he'd have something to play with. She could hear his laugh, a sneaky little chuckle that often led to a full-blown smoker's coughing choke, and it did make her laugh in spite of herself.

"Oh yes, your *time* in Asheville, back when you were *finding yourself* and, in the process, found a baby, too."

"Exactly," she said and looked over where Dillon was still sleeping in his little carrier. "Back when I got a degree and found out how good it felt to use my own brain." She spit the words as if to say that what had come out of Theresa's brain all those years raising her was stupid. "I'm just saying that I have always wondered if Mr. Graham . . . "

"Reverend. He was a reverend."

"If *Reverend* Graham would have had the same effect with the altar calls if he'd been five foot two, bald, and nearsighted." Miss Sassy Candyland laughed and then stared hard, wanting Theresa to take the bait and either break down in a laugh or a sob. That was the way it had always been with them—a laugh or a sob—and she wasn't going to give her the satisfaction of either if she could help it. She didn't even say how that pitiful person described would have nothing in common with Billy Graham.

Theresa bit her tongue and waited, watched Candy bend over double laughing and then plop into the kitchen chair, one big blue sneaker propped on the chair opposite, which is the way she had sat through childhood. Oscar had often joked that the fourth chair at the table was for Candy's foot, shoe going back and forth like a windshield wiper, though the leg of the old days was not decorated in such an awful, reptile-looking way. Oscar had also said he wanted a family of four and was sad when they realized that just wasn't going to happen. "But hey," he said when he caught her crying and thought *that* was why. "Our little Candy is like having two. She sure is."

"So, speaking of what I see out on the highway," Candy said, looking more like her old self with that dragon hidden, elbows on the table and her pale face propped in her hands; she looked more and more like Oscar, those sad dark eyes too big for her face. "They finally put a stem on that big peach water tower in Gaffney." They had laughed over that water tower for years because Oscar always said it looked just like a great big fanny. In fact, when Candy was little, she begged to stop so she could look longer—*the fanny, the fanny*, she screamed—and Oscar always stopped and let her stare at it and point at the big, crack-like crease. Obviously, they weren't the only people on I-85 to see the resemblance. "So now," she continued, "it looks like a big shiny fanny wearing a fig leaf." Candy said she wished her dad could see it; she wished he could see Dillon and know that she had a good job teaching at the junior high school, that she was independent and happy, that she found her path the way he always told her he hoped she would. She was always wishing Oscar alive again and there was a way, it left Theresa feeling like the back door was going to open any minute or that she would hear him in there flipping the channel and asking why they had 257 channels and not one of them worth a shit.

The thought of the big fanny did tickle Theresa, and she couldn't help but join in, the two of them sitting there at the table and laughing like some giant hand had come and turned back time, parted the turbulent seas and showed what might be a peaceful loving path before them, the path Oscar wanted so bad. For a second, they were there in that old Chevrolet wagon, Oscar's arm reaching across the front seat, fingers brushing her shoulder in that way he always did, like he wasn't quite sure if she wanted him there or not, and that made sense because she wasn't sure, but what she could count on was how he'd glance in the rearview and grin to see Candy hanging out the window and pointing at the water tower. Please stop, Candy would beg. *Please*, Theresa thought all those times a tenderness surged within herself, *please hold tight, keep this close*: Candy on Picture Day thinking she looked beautiful with a big chartreuse bow in her frizzy hair, Candy presenting her with a corsage made out of fried marbles and pipe cleaners on Mother's Day, Candy begging to curl up beside her and Oscar for one more TV show. She loved that one called *Full House* and another called *Who's the Boss?*, both households held in place by the men. Theresa had never thought of that until now and didn't want to think about what that meant; she preferred to think of how Candy was all curled up and chewing on the collar of her fluffy bathrobe, how Theresa did not tell her to stop doing that and did not resist when Candy pulled her arm in close and hugged. Of course, no sooner did she feel the surge and calm and think *please* than the waters rushed back in, blinding and choking and sweeping all that was tender away.

"How many 'planned accidents' do you think happen out there in the world?" she asked. "Speaking of that baby in the pan."

"What do you mean by that?"

"Oh, you know what I mean." She did her fingers in the air like quotes. "'A loss' without having to tell anyone or be responsible for it. You know. An 'accident.'"

"No. No, I don't know. I have no idea."

"Young women who claim appendicitis or those who 'accidentally' fall down a flight of stairs or 'accidentally' douche with Clorox."

"Stop! What an ugly thing to say."

"Ugly? You want to talk about what's ugly? Listen to what some of my eighth graders have been through. That sad miscarriage you keep staring at instead of looking at us is ugly. I have a sweet baby right there and you don't have time to watch him for fifteen minutes because you're watching *that*. What about *that baby* right there in the damn car seat? Your grandbaby. A living breathing baby instead of all those creepy stuffed things you have everywhere. They're what's *ugly*."

"It's a collection. I deserve something that's all my own." She went and stood in front of the shelves, arms crossed over her chest and head feeling light and yes, Dillon was cute, but who did he even look like? She told Faye that he had dark eyes like Candy, but Faye said what about his hair? She asked what the texture was and waited for Theresa to say something, like she might be some cosmetology person. *It feels like hair*, she said, *baby hair*, and then she worked hard to shift the attention to somebody whose daughter was trying to become a son, so maybe Faye would think about *that* hair.

Nothing made Theresa feel as good as to look out the window and see a new package outside her door, and when she was uncomfortable, that's what she thought about; everything seemed better, hopeful, and she would put it there on the coffee table and make herself wait like a child at Christmas. Sometimes she would wait until after she'd had dinner and a hot bath, hair pinned, pajamas on. She was careful to keep the box intact after it was opened, so she could keep it up in the attic with all the others. She loved the new smell and how real they all looked; she read aloud the certificate of authenticity, proud to know that this little creation was of a limited number and over the years would be more and more valuable and especially with the original box and certificate carefully preserved.

Faye said if you watched real close you could see the baby in the pan reaching out to whoever was filming it. She said it looked like it was trying to speak, to beg for its little life. She said some people who viewed this thought that baby was speaking in an unknown tongue like a little prophet there in the pan, but Theresa has yet to see all that and that's one reason why she keeps watching it over and over again. She hasn't seen but is afraid to admit it. She *wants* to see; she keeps hoping that eventually she will. Candy/Dandy/Zandy/Hateful kept asking why was she watching over and over and for one thing it didn't stop on its own but was fixed to keep repeating unless Theresa turned the computer off so she could not help that, she could not, and weren't there lots of things she could not help? Yes! *Damn. Damnation.* She is not a woman to cuss but *damn* and *double goddamn*. And what if Faye asked her that question, did you see the baby in the pan begging for its life? She was going to lie, what other choice was there? She's a believer after all and she did not want anyone questioning or doubting where she stands with the Lord.

"That thing isn't begging," Candy said. "Please. You want to see real begging? Do you?" And then she talked about neglected, abused children and God knows what on death row. "How about I send you some links to watch and read?"

"Leave me alone!" She closed the lid on the computer. Maybe when she came back she could see better what Faye said was happening. Sometimes it's just hard to see or know something. How can you *know*? She was just a girl that long-ago Sunday afternoon. She was on the sidewalk, pushing a doll in a buggy, stepping wide over the cracks and kicking leaves and pecans out of her way, when her grandmother's neighbor called out he needed her help. He said he'd dropped something valuable, a rare coin from his collection, and it had gone down that hole over there where the radiator used to be. He said he needed her thin little arm to reach way down there. Lean in, he said, lean all the way in. She was sorry she'd left her doll outside and was scared something would bite her hand down in the dark hole. There was dirt and what felt like spiderwebs, and she was afraid she'd never find it and she didn't; she reached and reached but she couldn't feel a thing. He said God makes us walk through darkness so we can get to the light and later her grandmother asked how she got so filthy and ran warm water into the tub. She said she needed a good soak in a tub, soap on her dirty little hand, and *how on earth did your hand get so dirty?* And here, now, take this soapy cloth and soap up yourself—you know what I mean. Wash (she said "warsh") yourself. And that same night they sat in her grandmother's small den watching the boxy television on those spidery legs—the antennae reaching out to Billy Graham there in fuzzy black and white with open arms. *Just as I am*, they sang, *oh lamb of God*, and the two things have been all merged and mangled up in her brain ever since no matter how fast she tried to live each day or how many precious creations she ordered to fill up the space or how many mission projects she participated in and she did participate, she did pray, she did give her money and her heart and her soul and so why won't they leave her alone?

She married Oscar and he was a good man—he really was. He might've smoked too much—the lung cancer is what killed him, after all—and he might've liked drinking more than most—something she would never tell Faye or anybody—but he did not have a temper and he did care about others. It wasn't his fault she didn't love him the right way and how could she have ever even known that. She wanted to love him that way; she tried to. She did her best, didn't she? There anchored to life in a sunbaked duplex, the roach motel beneath the sink looking as comfortable, the summer sun hot as Hades and that window unit barely a spit of air and nicotine-yellowed shades pulled low to block the light, but Oscar kept on and on, always working, always with an idea: a swing set and sandbox, a coat of paint. Then, when she complained there was not enough room, he found the house she has lived in ever since, a nice house, a solid house, handrails in case of ice. "A place you will feel safe," he had said and then later he said *but how could you*, face twisted in pain, when she, in a moment of anger, said words she could never call back.

Candy was in school and living in a rented apartment up in the mountains and it hit Theresa how all the doors of her life had slammed shut, and she felt trapped, desperate. He said, "What about my life? Did you ever think of my life?" He said, "Did you ever love me that way?" and she said yes, even though she wasn't sure. How can a person ever be sure?

"Did anybody ever pull your head toward his crotch when you didn't want to go?" Candy asked, up and ready to go another round. "Or pin you down and not let you up?"

"Of course not! Don't talk to me that way."

"Well then, let's call you blessed. But others aren't so fortunate." Candy kept right on talking, even though Theresa was trying to get away from her.

"Can I pee in private, please?" she yelled and locked herself in the bathroom, but Candy kept right on talking through the bathroom door, the back of which still had little hooks down low where Oscar put them when Candy was a child so she could hang her robe and towel there.

"Imagine the worst things you could call a woman and having those awful words spit into your face," Candy was saying, and Theresa flushed and then ran water in the sink. When pregnant that other time—Oscar didn't know—she slipped on the back steps and landed so hard she couldn't breathe for a second and as she lay there waiting to catch her breath, she made a wish she could get rid of the ache and grief she was always feeling. *Leave me alone* was her thought. *Please.* Her grandmother had said, a girl should never invite trouble. She tried her best to pray but all she could think was her grandmother saying how nobody should expect miracles, that God is on a party line and much of the time he's answering others with all kinds of whines and nonsense. It would be selfish to think he can always fix what's broken, and yet, the praying continues. Everybody's praying and some are getting answers and others aren't. Why does that one get cancer or a no-good husband and why is that one over there all draped in fur and easy living? Why is Faye Pitman living such an easy life? Is it because she guards the books and keeps up with who is *really needy* and spreads the word or video on what others need to see and know?

"What about the lives already here?" Candy asked as soon as Theresa came back into the kitchen. She was standing there with her hands on her hips in a know-it-all way. She would not shut her big, impudent, sassy mouth. "What about the kids in public school whose breakfasts have been taken away? Or the ones getting molested by people who are supposed to be watching out for them?"

"What about you be quiet. What about you quit torturing me!"

"Torturing? *You* feel tortured?"

"And how can you talk that way with your own baby sitting right there."

"Because I love him and I waited till I wanted him. There was never a doubt in my mind."

"Well, there was a doubt in somebody's mind, I suspect. You are *not* the virgin mother."

"No, I *chose* to have a baby, but I can also imagine someone having doubts; that's what people mean when they say 'openminded.' I can imagine the heartache a young woman might feel making a choice and I can imagine all the different circumstances, no two stories exactly the same. For all I know you didn't want me." Candy looked at Theresa like she knew something but that was impossible.

"Maybe I didn't." Theresa mimicked, using the sarcastic voice Oscar once said made his blood run cold; it surprised her how easily she lashed out. "But I had you, didn't I? So, there's your answer. Think about that."

"I have. Don't you think I felt your resentment? All the ways you believe you sacrificed yourself. You've never even said you loved me."

"Actions are louder than words."

"Not big on hugging either, except when it's something stuffed that comes with a certificate."

"Oh, sing another sad one," she said, and played an invisible violin, another thing Oscar said turned her into someone he didn't know. *That's just plain mean*, he had said. *Where does all that come from, Theresa? You act so cruel and hateful and then you pull God into it.* She was breathing hard and had to go and stand at the sink, run the water, reach her mind as far as it could go toward the sun. "All mothers feel that way and just think, where would you be if I'd spoiled and filled your head up with things that just weren't true. Where would you be if I hadn't let you be born?"

"I'm a mother and I don't feel that. And where would I *be*? My soul would have found another life, another home, maybe one where I was wanted. Maybe some angel or spirit guide would have said, hmmmm, let's put her over here in this womb, the one made ready for a baby and all the love they deserve."

"Angels don't work that way! Angels aren't silly fairies that do what you tell them to do. You can't believe what God says but you believe nonsense. Can't go to church but talk of 'spirit guide' like you're on a cruise somewhere, probably gnomes and witches and what have you like in cartoons and horror shows."

"*Et tu, Maman*?" Miss Candy Classroom Know-It-Goshdamn-All said and pointed to the TV in the kitchen tuned to a man in face paint with horns and they were talking about pornography at the Pizza Hut, which sounded horrible to Theresa. Who would even think of having sex there at the Pizza Hut and with children! Faye Pitman said she loved a Super Supreme thin crust, but never again would it touch her lips until she knew some poor child had not been harmed there in the back room when her pizza was baking.

"My soul would have served a purpose if it taught you a lesson. Perhaps you would have gone forward and been able to lead a *happy* life, one not so steeped in bitterness." Candy stopped and went and stood right beside her, right in slapping distance. "And you know what I would've liked about that? Then my daddy's life wouldn't have been so *tortured*."

"Oh, your soul. Where do you get all that trash, the fortune teller? And your daddy was never tortured."

"My religious beliefs make just as much sense as yours do. The God I believe in encourages people to use their brains, God-given organs that science has taught us how to best care for. I wanted my baby and I'm thinking about having another before my eggs go bad."

"And what Tom, Dick, or Harry will provide the fertilizer?"

"Or Rashid or Ahmud."

"I said what Tom, Dick, Harry, or *Sambo*."

"Nice. Did you learn that from Faye, too, or did God and the Klan send you a telegram?"

Theresa took a deep breath, still staring out into the yard. Last week Candy had brought over an old *National Geographic* to show her a picture of what somebody said Jesus *really* looked like and it was nothing like any picture of Jesus she had ever seen. Theresa told her he looked more like that man that collects their garbage and can't speak English, and Candy said well, that made sense because Jesus was also a trash collector—recycling lost and trashed souls. She had stood there fanning that magazine in her face and then added, *And this is what he looked like.*

"So did I teach you anything you believe?" Theresa didn't dare turn to see the reaction.

"Yes." Candy paused a long pause and Theresa focused on her hands there in the running water. "One of your many diets made a lot of sense. You said we should eat like we lived in the book of Deuteronomy and it was actually healthy."

"What?" she said and turned off the water. She hadn't thought of the Deuteronomy diet in years, and how Oscar made them laugh when he came to the dinner table wearing a bedsheet and sandals and a Christmas wreath on his head. Candy's baby was starting to stir and make some noises.

"It was like the Mediterranean diet, you know, lots of fruits and nuts and antioxidants and it was about the same time you got your color wheel."

"And do you believe that? That some of us look better in one color than another because of our season or did you think that was stupid?"

"Actually, I do believe that—you're winter and I'm spring—and of course, Deuteronomy was so much better than all your other diets. Remember the Hotdog/Banana/boiled egg diet—basically nine hundred calories a day and what about when you lived on bacon and cheese and pork rinds and then began smelling bad?"

"Can't we keep it pleasant for once? I didn't get an education like you. I wanted one but I didn't get that, but I have worked hard my whole life and tried to be a good person."

"I know. You didn't get an education because you were having me. I've heard it my whole life but it's not too late. Go back to school."

"Oh yes. How simple." This was another conversation they'd had, and it never went well.

"What? Do you want me to give you some cash?" Candy said. "Or a pint of blood? We could pray about it, or you could sell all those dolls and make a fortune."

"Don't mock me and don't you mess with my collection!" Theresa ran over and snatched the doll named Lisette out of Candy's hand. Lisette's little face was all scrunched up like she was about to cry and that was exactly what Dillon was doing with sound.

"I remember my friend, Ginger, seeing all of this and saying she had always wondered what kind of person bought all those things out of the magazines," Candy said. By then, Dillon was red-faced and screaming, bouncing on Candy's hip where Theresa could see the beginning of yet another tattoo of God only knows what. She was not about to ask.

"I never liked her," Theresa said instead. "A bad influence with that brassy hair and tight pants and hot-to-trot look. She could have just hung a price tag around her neck."

"Well, now she's a cardiologist and active in the Episcopal church where she leads the prayer all the time. You never liked any of my friends," Candy said. "And if my friends could manage to be around you, then these creepy-ass dolls scared them off." Dillon stopped crying and smiled right at Theresa like he thought that might be funny. Candy lifted one of the monkey dolls and shook it back and forth and it made Theresa furious even though it made him laugh, those black eyes shining.

"Stop it. And don't touch them. It says right here: *not a toy a collectible*," she said. Theresa had all three little monkeys, Annabelle, Clementine, and Coco. Little monkey babies that look so real you can't believe it. She wanted all three, like see and hear and speak no evil. Little Coco has big ears and reminds her of Oscar's mother, and she has all seven dwarves with little toboggans with their names embroidered. She'd gotten all seven—$39.99 each—and loved looking forward to the arrival. It was exciting each time to find that box there on the front steps, the nice mailman who always wished her a nice day. She could spend hours with each new one.

"Well, they aren't toys," she said again and pointed to where a child from next door had messed with Clementine's eye when Theresa wasn't looking and she has had a time getting it fixed back just right so it doesn't look cross-eyed, her gnarled, arthritic thumbs fumbling to undo the damage done. Clementine has a little pacifier and hairy little legs not unlike Theresa's own as a girl. It was devastating when a boy in school—Perry Parker— told her she had legs like a chimpanzee and she never got over it even though he had jug ears and pigeon toes and grew up to be an alcoholic. To think he made her ashamed of her little hairy legs all those years ago, but here on the little monkey doll it looks cute.

"Speaking of the right to life," Candy Corn who could *not shut up* said, "let's talk elder care. Last time I saw your friend, Marie, she looked a lot like that baby in the pan, all curled up and dying."

"Stop!"

"I've noticed you never go see *her* anymore."

"You don't know what I do. You don't know who I see."

"Or what about Dad? He really looked a lot like the baby in the pan there at the end."

"Stop!"

"Maybe Ashton-Drake or whoever could do a whole series of elderlies. Here's Marie, press this button and she struggles to breathe; open her mouth and find the lifelike wads of food packed away that no one has bothered to clear. And here's little deaf and blind Gertie Andrews whose Depend has not been changed in hours."

"Stop."

"Or I know. What about the Death Row series? Little orange jumpsuits and lifelike wrinkles, complete with certification of false convictions and nightly rapes."

"You think you know everything, and you know nothing," Theresa raised her voice and Dillon smiled at her with his mouth hanging open, a string of drool out of one side. The last time she'd gone to see Marie, it was clear that it upset her; Marie didn't want people seeing her looking so bad.

"Here's Oscar, lift his little jammies and see the bedsores, so lifelike you expect them to ooze." Candy says it all in a singsong voice that makes Dillon laugh again. "He can be yours for three easy payments of $39.99."

"Why don't you just say you hate me," Theresa said. "Why don't you just say it?"

"I think you want me to say it so you can say it back. Do unto others, right?" Candy fastened Dillon back into his carrier and started gathering her things. "You see, I think you hate life. I think you talk about the baby in the pan because it lets you hate. You can hate the woman who put the baby in the pan and anybody who helped her. And what skin is it off of you? The baby in the pan is no more alive than that room full of creepy dolls and yet you spend more time and money on them than you do your own grandson. You hate life. You've always hated life. Answer that altar call."

"Get out!" Theresa ran and waited in the kitchen until she heard them drive away; then she slammed the front door so hard, a vase fell from a shelf and shattered, and she felt just like she did that other time, wanting to cry but something cold and hard keeping her from it, Oscar asking about *his* life, did she ever think of his life, or *what about Candy* he asked, *what about our baby?* and what about that long-ago day that still made her shake her head from side to side when her grandmother handed her that soapy rag and said where on earth have you been and why did you leave your nice doll out there on the street where it could've been took and *look at your dirty dirty little hand*, and the baby in the pan *did* die and God only knows what they did with it. Faye didn't tell that part, if there's a little tombstone somewhere to remember it, if anybody cared. Did anybody care? When she lay there at the bottom of the steps that time, she thought how she hated her life and all that had happened to make her hate and she made a wish and said a prayer just like she did that time she was called to reach her arm down into that small, dark hole, her cheek pressed hard against the cold, dusty floor, a heavy hand on the back of her head and she could hear water running in the kitchen where the man's wife was washing dishes and singing with the radio—what was the song, she tried to hear the song—*keep reaching, baby, reach, reach*—and it all got merged and mangled in her brain, the love and the hate, a messy tangle of reaching and praying.

✳ Filling Station

With the approach of his sixtieth birthday, Ben McCallum found himself thinking a lot about death. He was always a little behind the curve getting where he wanted to be and so it made sense that his bout of "middle-aged crazy" would come not in the middle but closer to retirement and the home stretch. He had no cravings of the normal clichés—cars, boats, women, gambling; his mortal craving was simply for peace of mind. He longed for the kind of safe comfort he remembered from a brief time in childhood when he lived out in the country with his grandparents. He craved small spaces and simple equations with clear answers. Then the FOR RENT sign appeared like a message.

He had always been attracted to seemingly forgotten places—
rooms above garages, or downtown businesses, small, desert-
ed-looking houses of tar paper or cinder blocks. Sometimes he
passed such places and allowed himself to linger in an imagined
life, to follow the trail of a sweat-slicked child—eyes adjusting from the bright daylight to the darkened interiors, where
he might stretch out on the cool wooden floor in front of a box
fan and doze off. A rusty screen door, stale country smells he
knew from his own childhood. He imagined a quilt-covered cot
and leftovers on the stove. The house of his childhood was still
there, just beyond where the old drive-in theater had been—the
overgrown marquee with all kinds of graffiti about what was
"Coming Soon": Jesus / the end of time / Tony and Sue / higher
taxes—and Bernie's Seafood, recently closed and boarded up, a
place he loved as a kid because there was a huge aquarium filled
with giant goldfish and a collection of other things people had
managed to put in there, an old rusty cap gun and a cigarette
lighter and the bride and groom off the top of a wedding cake.
There was a little sign taped to the glass and written in a bub-
bly way like the fish said it: PLEASE RESPECT MY HOME, but
it seemed every time he went, there was something new down
there in the gravel—handcuffs, lipstick, snuff tin.

His grandparents' house was now a convenience store—they
would have said *fillin' station*—with a single gas pump so old it
didn't take credit cards, a faded *Esso* sign and a cardboard cut-
out of Richard Petty that looked like he had the shakes whenever
a car passed. But, if Ben ignored the gas pump and signs and just
focused on the distant treeline and listened to the passing train,
he could almost conjure his grandparents in their old spots—her

in the kitchen and him perched on that concrete stoop—the same one still there.

He wanted to escape. But from what? That is the question he imagined someone would ask of him: *What more could you possibly want?* He had a thriving business—a billboard with his name on it welcomed people into the city limits—nice house, charming wife, two grown daughters seemingly happy in their own lives. He was on a couple of boards in town, had run a marathon in support of cancer, walked miles for Alzheimer's and autism, seen his grandparents and then parents through old age and death along with the man he gave credit for helping him find his way in life. His high school shop teacher, Mr. Alton Ward, was a role model and father figure, offering support and encouragement at crucial make-or-break times, and Ben had never forgotten that.

"He's dying," Mrs. Ward had called to tell him. "In case you want to say goodbye." He had only rented the room the week before and now more than ever he needed the space.

Mr. Ward was one of those teachers that students talked about in positive ways, imitating his swagger and repeating the funny sayings and stories. He told jokes and gave a lot of advice, something that drew boys who had no interest at all in shop to sign up for his class. Kids ended the term with crappy-looking tables and jewelry boxes but lots of good stories to tell like that long ago spring day he went off on Sansabelt slacks. "Sansabelt slacks are for slackasses," he said. "A man needs a belt—think what you can do in a pinch here in shop— hold those boards together, keep your mufflers on, and from the looks of what you kids are driving, that's needed. Also a

belt is for protection—keep the wild girls out unless you're prepared to take care of things—right? Or swing that son of a bitch
in self-defense like that Lee character you're all talking about.
Sansabelts are for pussies." It was the early seventies and they'd
all seen *Enter the Dragon* several times; even Mr. Ward had
seen it, though he still maintained that a belt with a good, solid
buckle—his was brass with a big hammer on it—was a good
match for nunchucks or whatever, any day of the week. He said
his wife didn't like the movie at all and that was fine because she
had sure hauled his ass to some bad ones.

Ben's grandparents' closest neighbor—down the road and across
from an old country cemetery—had been a woman named Sadie,
and though she was long gone, Ben thought of her daily because
her house was also still standing. There was a big tractor tire
filled with flowers in the front yard, the only sign of domestic
life left on that lonely stretch of road, but probably not for long
given the steady outgrowth of neighborhoods and trailer parks.
In recent years, Sadie's son, Roland, had lived there and was
often on the porch in the late afternoon, a punching bag hanging on the front porch and boxing gloves on his hands. He was
several years older than Ben, a divorced insurance investigator,
and they'd always waved at each other when he passed by. He
once made the comment that his mother and Ben's grandparents
were still neighbors and he pointed across the road to the small
overgrown cemetery that dated back to the 1800s. Now he was
buried there as well. Ben hadn't been in the cemetery in a while
even though he had good intentions. The last time he went, the
litter—beer cans and liquor bottles, condoms and hypodermics

left on and behind tombstones—had left him feeling disgusted and helpless, though lately there had been groups of prisoners cleaning up the ditches and surrounding area so he was hopeful things might look a little better. He had also planned to stop and visit Roland, talk about how it used to be, but too late now, another sad addition to the *dead too soon* list.

Mr. Ward would never get away with saying all that he said these days, and he had been even more colorful out on the baseball field where he sometimes assisted the coach, chewing tobacco and spitting like a pro. His class was an education in so many ways, and Ben had spent the past thirty-five years hearing him in his head with advice and directions, laughing every time he thought of Sansabelt slacks, which was usually every morning when he got dressed and fastened the silver monogrammed belt buckle his mother had given him for graduation. It came on an alligator belt, his mother clearly wanting him to look more like all the college-bound guys in his class. Alligator belt and little alligators on their shirts. She had had her dreams for him and he was sorry she didn't live to see how much money he had made just doing what he loved and something that came so naturally. A natural gift.

Alton Ward had told Ben he had *a natural gift* for building and creating things, at a time when very little in life was working out for him, and he'd invited him to help on some community projects where they rebuilt houses damaged by storms or just age and abandonment. Ben thought every day how he could trace everything back to that moment and it was why he wanted to be there for the man as he was dying. Even Alton's wife had said that surely Ben had things he needed to be doing, and he did, but he had missed his own father's death—too many miles between them to get there in time—which made this goodbye even more important.

Ben had owned his own business for twenty years, something else he attributed to all he had learned from Mr. Ward. He was a contractor and had more work than he could possibly do, his days spent talking to people who wanted enormous spaces with everything of the highest grade—bluestone terraces and marble counters; people who wanted full-grown trees transported to make a brand-spanking-new house appear like an old histor- ical landmark. He and his wife had all of that. He had even gone years when he rarely even thought of his own childhood and all of the differences in the two ways of life, how *he* was the child he often saw feeling his way into and through that darkened tiny house in search of a cool place to rest or to hide if there were chores or homework to be done or loud voices from another room during that period of time when he and his parents lived there. He wanted to be by himself in his room, to read and imagine himself in a life more like the one he was now living, though the boyhood dream was one richly populated with animals—a whole team of beagles or coonhounds like in *Where the Red Fern Grows*, one that looked like *Old Yeller*, and perhaps a horse or two. His father left not long after that time, living a couple of towns over and then a couple of states away, and Ben and his mother found a small house in town near the elementary school and started all over again. Still, that small country home was the place he always went back to in his mind.

So, what was he missing and in need of escaping? His marriage had been a storybook, high school romance that survived her going away to school, the birth and raising of two daughters, seeing elderly parents along the way, but at some point within the daily patterns, the path forked and their desires became a meandering stream of you buy this and I'll buy that, you do this and I'll do that, you choose here, I'll choose there, a constant adjustment to keep the balance yet each tip of the scale lengthened the distance between them. They were always polite but then when the kids were grown and out on their own, their differences led to what felt contrary and then combative, even vindictive at times. A distant chill had set in, shrouding every conversation, something he felt on the job as well, judgments and demands interrupting his sleep.

"This just will not do," he heard a zillion times a year, some fancy shoe pointing to where one stone was spaced a little differently. There were people who actually asked that it all be ripped out and redone if only a fraction off. There was no room for human error these days, not at work and not at home. The little bit he knew about art or literature would argue that often what *is* interesting *is* what makes something different or unique—the little flaw, the chip, the birthmark.

Just recently, a couple—at least twenty years younger—was overseeing everything he or his crew touched. Every brick laid and every nail driven. It was exhausting. "How are you choosing which stone goes where?" the guy kept asking. Rumor had it that he was in on some ground floor of yet another virtual this or that, cashed in and made a fortune and spent his days strutting around the pool or complaining about a lack of perfection.

"By the way," the guy had said just the day before, "where do you get these people who work for you? Does anybody speak English?" Even though many had grown up right there and spoke as well as he did, the asshole slowed to enunciate. Ben had seen the men react, the shake of a head, the laughter when Sam pretended he was deaf, leaning forward with a strained expression, hand cupped to his ear. They all laughed at Ben's own pathetic Spanish duo/babble, which seemed in good humor, but who knew? He was trying his best.

The couple doing the renovation invited him in for lunch—they said—though probably they really wanted to talk about more ideas and how to shave pennies from a million-dollar job. They invited him in while the crew was expected to keep working, but he refused; instead, he drove the two miles out of the subdivision and onto old 301, where life was considerably different. It was a part of the county still untouched by the gentrification that moved like a wash of varnish over the past.

This area would remain untouched thanks to the floodplain and low swampland stretching to the coast. He had grown up in town near the elementary school his own children had attended, but his own childhood was one of time travel. Middle-class 1960s town life with his mom and then out in the country where it was more like the thirties or forties, his grandparents shaped by the Depression and living an old farm life just as they had growing up. Days dictated by sunrise and sunset, scraps of string and foil saved for later, hard work all week, quiet Sundays. No close neighbors to critique and complain.

His grandmother believed you should do nothing on Sunday and did all the cooking Saturday night. Sunday was a day of rest and she wouldn't even let him use scissors to clip from the funny papers or use a hammer or nails or dig a hole. He couldn't go swimming, and though there was a lot he missed on those long Sunday afternoons, he also loved the world being at rest. He remembered hearing a girl in high school—she had grown up in New York—say, *This Bible belt is strangling the hell out of me*, something he has thought of many times over the years with his own sensations of suffocation. Lots of words—*I pray I pray*—and so little substance.

His grandparents' house had been sold and turned into a store in the early seventies, that old pump out front sometimes working and sometimes not, dusty cans on shelves, a Coke cooler so old it vibrated on the old linoleum floor, the same floor his grand-mother had swept daily, and each time he was there, it was hard not to look for dents and flaws he would recognize.

Now, he went every day. The sloping concrete driveway was the same, a square cement block where the well had been. Every day a soda and a bag of potato chips, a stale sandwich already made and wrapped up by the cash register. He could not place the ethnicity of the dark-complexioned young woman behind the counter and wouldn't have dared to try for fear of insult. She had a tough-girl look about her even though there was not one feature that would make her so. She was scrawny with a poof of bleached hair like a dandelion.

One day when he stopped in, she looked up and said "Oh, you." Her words were high-pitched, long, flattened syllables that seemed to linger too long on her tongue, not what he'd expected at all.

"Yeah, been working down in the mansion district." He pointed down the highway to the new neighborhood, the entrance attended by someone in a uniform, and was embarrassed by the false ring of his own voice, trying to imply he lived a life more like hers and ashamed of his own truth. "What a bunch of shits."

"Hmmm," she didn't look up but continued scribbling a column of figures, adding and crossing out. "Some real lucky shits."

"Oh not necessarily," he said and she looked up then, smart enough to check out his hands, the neat, clean nails unlike those of some on his crew. She glanced out to his truck, his own golf clubs visible in the cab. He was in work clothes and boots, but they were nice work clothes and boots—his wife always made sure of that—and her eye fixed on his belt buckle his mother was so proud to have purchased over forty years ago.

"Hmmm," she said again with a smirk and let out a fake laugh, as if to say, "Look who's talking." "Well if you have to be unlucky, I suspect that's still the way to go." She didn't smile, just went back to her scribbling. She wore blue eye shadow, little tails drawn out from her eyes like a cat, and she had several rings on each hand, big, ornate rings that dwarfed her fingers, nails bitten down to skin. She reminded him of half the girls he had grown up with—different styles but same image—some of them drifting from high school even before graduation—babies, husbands, minimum-wage jobs.

"My name's Ben," he extended his hand, but she ignored it. "My grandparents used to live here. When I was a kid, a large elm tree was right where the pump is." He touched the black screen of the door where there was now a COME AGAIN sign. "Same door, too," he added. "I really think it is."

"Okay," and she turned her attention to the door behind her, where there were the muffled sounds of a radio or television. "You need anything else?"

When the FOR RENT sign went up in the upstairs window, he could not get it off his mind. For three days he drove past, each time hesitating and staring up at the little dark window looking down over the pumps. He had the strangest feeling that if he could be up there looking down he might understand more about all those times he had stayed there. He had always been sorry they sold it, but what recourse was there, when his grandfather died and his grandmother needed nursing care. By then he was in junior high school, living with a single mother, and his father was remarried and living in Georgia.

Now he had a picture-perfect bungalow refurbished to a tee and a decorator wife who worked out of a converted carriage house. Their daughters, now married, had grown up with whole little universes for rooms—murals painted by a local artist, one a fairy kingdom and the other a rain forest. The bathroom had clouds on the ceiling and lush flowers on the walls. He lived in a "good" section of town, with the "good" elementary school. He had in-ground sprinklers and a yard service and a team of women in pink shirts who showed up every Monday to clean.

On impulse, he asked, and next thing he knew, he was mounting those familiar stairs, hand gripping the railing, and then walking around the tiny space while she stood in the doorway, the key ring jangling as she passed it back and forth between her hands. The room was much smaller than he remembered, tiny sink and toilet hidden behind a curtain. Sloping floors, cracked plaster; the old milk glass overhead fixture was the same. The dormer that overlooked the pumps was the only window that had not been nailed and painted shut. This was the room where he had slept as a child, sometimes with his mother in the twin bed beside him, but usually he was there alone, with his grandparents in their room just below. The room cost less than it did to board the family dog, and yet it felt more like home than anywhere he'd been in decades. Sure the furniture was drab and rickety, but that had also been true in his childhood. His grandmother had brightened it up with quilts on the bed and flowers in the window, doilies she had made herself on the tables.

"Well?" the girl said, still in the doorway.

"Yes. I'll take it."

"Cash?"

"Yeah sure." He stepped forward and extended his hand and this time she took it, her grip aggressive in its firmness. "If that's what you prefer."

"I like cash. You can pay weekly if you want but I'm hoping you might rent for at least a couple of months."

"Sure. Of course." He paused, tried to make eye contact, but she was already heading back down the narrow stairs that opened to the back lot littered with recyclables and old tires. He followed her, the stairs and his descent so familiar that he felt a moment of disorientation, overwhelmed by sudden memories of his grandparents and young mother—twenty years younger than he was now—then repeated his question. "So you prefer weekly?"

"Yeah, that's best." Her eyes were dark brown, nearly black, and she had caked-on lashes, like some child playing dress-up. "People never stay long." He could see clearly in this light that nature would never have intended her to have blonde hair, her brows dark and severely arched. She wore a ripped-up T-shirt from a Stones concert.

"So you like the Stones?"

"Who doesn't?" She shook her head and smirked as if to say *what an idiot.*

He knew his wife wanted him to think that she was having an affair and by now, for all he knew she was. That was her way, nothing direct, always a trick of sorts. It wouldn't have occurred to her to ask what was bothering him, to say, *You seem so distant, let's talk.* It was a common enough story, if his suspicions were accurate, the neighbor they'd seen through a painful divorce needing time and attention. But for Ben the more upsetting part was that they had made fun of those people for years; after every neighborhood gathering for drinks, they entertained each other for days with the jokes and ridicule. The pretension, the fabricated tales and name-dropping. They had even staged little predictions in the past; name a movie star and see what happened. *It's like when I was in the airport and Jack Nicholson needed my help at the kiosk.* He was a mortgage banker and it seemed everywhere he had ever ventured in life he had found the rich and the famous in need of his help. *It's like when I was in Nashville, standing at a urinal singing and who came out of the stall but Johnny Cash, saying "Encore, Buddy."* (What the hell?) When alone they had referred to him as Forrest Gump and to his wife as BOF (Bride of Frankenstein), big, scared-looking eyes and hair spiked and harsh, face powdery and pasty. They laughed at the names of their children, all either long, sexless surnames or what sounded like tools, *Blade* or *Rake* (or *Hoe*, his wife had added on a particularly funny night). Were those really better times or were they just finding common ground in gossip as so many do—that desperate artificial bond of gossip and ridicule. "If your joy is at the expense of another," his grandmother once said, "then that is not joy." She had always been in his head—*haste makes waste, idle hands are the devil's workshop, this much laughter will soon lead to tears.*

And the laughter *had* turned to tears too many nights to count. Maybe the most disturbing fact of all was that he didn't care. In the beginning he did, an ego thing, but then he didn't and instead more and more found his attention on his grandparents' house and the decline of his teacher. When Mr. Ward was moved to hospice care, Ben went every day, often finding a ballgame on television if there was one to be seen. Ben could never repay his presence in those high school years, a grownup who loved woodworking and baseball and went to all the high school games. Mr. Ward believed Pete Rose should be forgiven and allowed in the Hall of Fame, something he and his wife, Loris, bantered back and forth about. She said that Pete Rose might've done better if he'd gone with someone more age appropriate. "Pete's crime was marrying somebody in diapers when he was already having denture woes and knee trouble," she said, "am I right?" She had a way of staring that left Ben feeling like she knew his thoughts and everything bad he'd ever done.

"What do you know about Pete Rose?" Mr. Ward said, his voice weak and barely a whisper.

"I know," she said. "I know enough."

Mr. Ward said he'd die easier if he knew Pete was forgiven. Another time he asked Ben if he believed in forgiveness. Ben said he guessed it depended on what had been done, and then was surprised to learn that they had a son he'd never mentioned and who hadn't been home in years. Mr. Ward didn't say anything more but it seemed in those last frantic mumblings—*Get in the truck, where's my belt? Don't look at me that way, boy*—that might have been what was on his mind.

During those last days, Ben spent his time either at the hospital or up in the room at his grandparents' house. He would climb the stairs, pour a drink from a flask he brought with him, and try to remember all those things the years had blurred. He could hear the radio from the office down below, the old beagle whining and straining on a piece of frayed rope. Cash register opening and closing. *You've done so well for yourself*, people often said. *Done so well for a boy like you.* His wife kept asking where he was all the time, surely not at the hospital all that time.

When he was in that place, he felt close to what had been missing all those years. Like Loris, there was so much he didn't know, but what he *did* know when sitting in that small room was what it felt like to be loved. This is where he had felt loved. Perhaps it was that simple.

Sometimes the woman came outside and he watched her. She sat on the concrete slab between the gas tanks and stared off into the dark woods, westward where the sky was still pink. The man who appeared most nights looked worn and much older than she was. There was a bitterness in his voice when he spoke to her in short commands and she followed like an obedient dog. They always looked up and he stepped back, hopefully hidden. It occurred to him that she had been in here; there was always the feeling that the space belonged to someone else and he found himself imagining just that—her face wiped clean of makeup, curled up on the sofa and drifting off to sleep.

He liked to think she was watching the sunset as she sat there, that, like him, she felt that melancholic yet peaceful dip each time the sun disappeared, another day finding closure. Or had she just been waiting for the man in the blue pickup, a child's single sneaker in the bed of the truck.

Then another day, there was the child who belonged to the shoe, a girl four or five stretched out on a blanket in the back of the truck staring up at the sky. He felt her eyes on his face, as if reading his thoughts, but he knew better, hidden there by the dark mesh. She lay, her right hand curled around something, feet bare. His daughter had carried a doll around in her pocket for years and if anyone asked what was happening in there, she had a wealth of information.

Godamnit, the voice below echoed through the walls, the very plaster trembling. The child was lying in the back of the truck, frozen, face turned toward the yelling. A slam / a slap. Should he intervene? Should he call 911? He stared at his cell where his wife had already called him twice. His absences were making her nervous, each day more and more so. I was with Mr. Ward, he said each time. Mr. Ward is dying.

The voices were getting louder, the child now on her side, thumb in her mouth. The only time he ever called 911 was a long-ago Thanksgiving when they lived in South Carolina. It was warm enough that people had their windows open and with this came the overload of vignettes—classical music, gospel, reggae, televised football and children playing, threads and filaments of life on the air and then the slaps and shouts—all the words you never want to be called—from an apartment across the way and it seemed all other sounds stopped, like birds when a snake appears. A pot came through a window and then a baby's plastic lawn-mower—the one with the little popcorn balls that his girls had pushed—and with it a shriek and child's cry. When the police arrived, they circled the building and led away a woman with a bloodied nose and bruised eye, a toddler holding her hand, then the man, belt unbuckled and dangling, shirt unbuttoned, shaking his head, hands raised palms up like he might've carried an invisible tray. He acted like he hadn't done a thing. He acted like a caring father, reaching to straighten the little boy's T-shirt. They cuffed him and put him in the back of the car and then came to Ben's door there in full view to identify him as the caller. He recognized the guy, someone who did maintenance in the complex, had even helped Ben when the washer was off balance, a man who smacked Dentyne and whistled a tune from a Disney movie he said his boy liked to watch. Before dusk that day, the family returned, all charges dropped except of course the one now against Ben for calling the cops, man and wife both staring at his door with anger, a look that said *mind your own fucking business.*

He was reaching for the phone when he heard the store door slam. The man swung open the door of the driver's side and stared up at the windows, shook his head and lit a cigarette. After what seemed an uncomfortably long pause, he got in and cranked the engine, revving hard on the gas several times before driving away, the child rolled to one side like a rag doll and the cardboard Petty shaking all over. Had he forgotten that the child was there? When the truck was gone, the woman came back out and sat there on the curb, lit a cigarette. One false flick and she could blow up the whole place. She craned her neck, sliver of moon and then up at his window. When he walked outside, she was still there, her eyes puffy, a cigarette burned to ash between her thin fingers. His phone had five messages—*where are you? when will you be home?* He had installed the neighbor's terrace and now he imagined the two of them out there sharing a drink in the cool darkness while they watched the driveway for his return.

"Are you okay?" he asked.

"Do I look okay?" Her makeup was smudged and hands shaking.

"No. You don't." He sat down beside her, careful to keep his distance. The beagle strained and whined and pulled at his rope to come between them.

"Let me ask you one goddamned thing." She paused and he nodded, waited, but then it was clear she changed her mind.

"What?"

"Forget it." She stubbed out her cigarette and then tossed the butt behind her into the parched shrubbery and sighed. He knew he should try to say something but felt frozen in the minute, incapable of even standing up. "Look." She turned and stared at him now. "Just don't go bringing men up there, okay?"

That's what she thought? Now he laughed. Now he knew that his suspicions were correct and that she had nosed around—the man, too, probably—and they had made assumptions about his life from his grandparents' things he had brought into the space, lamp with an old-timey lace shade and a pale pink shawl his grandmother kept at the foot of her bed, some books—Winston Churchill and Abraham Lincoln, both of whom, his grandfather had said, shared the dark cloud he knew so well. He had his grandmother's Bible with various pages marked with pieces of yarn and a book she had loved with pictures of all the local birds and wildflowers that he had given her one long ago Christmas when he was in high school. People put on goggles and visited places virtually these days, hours spent that way, so what was the difference? For him, that space was like entering Google Earth, visiting a place of the past only to see someone in the window. Was it his mother? His younger self? Was it his grandfather, whose sad view of the world was feeling more and more true? *How*, he had asked Ben on several occasions, *could anyone with a heart and a brain not be depressed?*

Now, her jaw quivered, anger or shame he couldn't tell.

"I'm not interested in men."

"What then?"

"I don't know." His certainty about his own uncertainty hit him like a cold wall of water. He knew it was about feeling loved but the equation seemed too difficult to even begin solving. He wanted to ask about the man, that child. It was clear now that she was even younger than he'd thought. "I spent so much time here as a child and feel like I lost something."

"Oh yeah? Everybody can name that tune." She stared out toward the street. "Looking for the magic rainbow and little unicorn. You don't belong here and he doesn't like it."

"I see."

"I would've sworn you were queer."

"Sorry to disappoint," he said, and she lit another cigarette. "That'll stunt your growth."

"Nothing left to stunt," she said. "And I didn't mean queer as an insult. Queers don't hit on you." His phone rang and she jumped. "Give me a heart attack why don't you?" She blew out a long trail of smoke. "So answer it."

"Nah, I'll deal with that later," he said.

"I know *that* story, too." she said. "Boy do I know that one."

In the days following, his wife was working hard to connect with him, planning things that would keep him home. She wanted to have a big neighborhood party, said it had been ages since they had done something fun or gotten to know some of the new people. *I need you,* she kept saying, *so much to get ready.* She was scurrying around behind him in a black bra and tight elastic shorts that looked painful to put on, puffing and pulling, body shining like a thick coat of armor, like those sand crabs he used to love to dig up on the shore when the waves receded. That's what she reminded him of, a sand crab, scurrying along, first this way and then that, or maybe a pill bug—what his grandparents called roly-polies—little prehistoric-looking thing that rolled up when confronted.

There were lanterns, expensive wine, and meager little bites of food served by people in uniform who he was sure had better things to do than wait for him to slurp a thimble of soup. The party went on way too long—celebrity sightings, McGillicuddy Montezuma's SAT scores, the renovation, the vacation, the blah and the blah and the blah. He was tempted to get his keys and leave but then she was there asking him to please stay home, she *needed* him, they needed to talk. Too much to drink, the moon sliced right in half, and for a moment he trusted her and could imagine lying in the dark making jokes about it all. Call it a pause before all the difficult things that would happen, split accounts and furniture tagged, their daughters—even though grown and in their own lives—reduced to their angriest eleven-year-old selves, the family time capsule waiting for another fifty years suddenly as worthless as the metal container it came with in 2000. And what had he even wished in that uneducated moment? That the computers not stop working as threatened? That his children would always be happy and healthy? Could he have wished the NY skyline would never change or that democracy would never be threatened? He probably made a wish about sports: to win the March Madness bracket, that Tom Brady play until he turned sixty, maybe he even wished for Pete Rose to be forgiven.

Then Mr. Ward died and it was all downhill from there. He helped arrange the funeral and delivered the eulogy; he helped poor Loris Ward—more rattled than ever—handle all the paperwork and make call after call to the son in Canada who finally answered and said with little to no emotion *maybe now she'll leave*. There was brief marriage counseling and a legal separation and a house on the market. When Ben finally returned to his little room, he knew before entering that something had happened. Ransacked. Stripped clean. There was only the shabby furniture that had been there. He stood in the center of the room and marveled at the emptiness. He took a deep breath and stared up at the light fixture, then took one last look out the window overlooking the street, walked down the narrow staircase and handed her the key.

"You been robbed I suspect."

"Yes." He reached for his wallet, counted out the bills, this week, next, two more.

"I didn't set you up."

"Never thought you had."

"They stole my radio." She followed him outside and he felt the glare from up above, someone already there in the window. "I'm sorry. I really am."

"Yeah, Me, too."

"You shouldn't have stayed gone so long." She stepped closer. "Or maybe you shouldn't've come at all."

✳ Confessional

The confessional did not catch their eye at first. It looked like a part of the dark woodwork in the antique shop or like an old mahogany ticket booth. The dark mesh screen of the opening was rusted, years of dampened breath of all who had knelt and whispered there. *It's had many, many lives*, the shop owner told them. She was barely five feet tall, with close-cropped orange hair and round green glasses. She stood with her hands deep in her trouser pockets and swayed to and fro as if on the deck of a ship while reciting the history.

It was Italian in origin, probably carved in Florence, and somehow it had found its way across the ocean and then landed in the chapel of a small Southern coastal town that nearly washed away in 1954 with Hurricane Hazel, a catastrophic Category 4 that devastated the area. *A miracle it survived*, she said, *a total miracle*. But, she continued, it was not enough to save that little church, especially as the Catholics (a very small number to begin with) dwindled; the building was razed—a convenience store is there now—and the pews went everywhere, no telling how many entryways in the Carolinas have one—and the confessional, this magnificent prize of artistry, became part of a local bar called Hoho's Haven, where things were stored out of sight along with cases of empty bottles and broken stools. Hoho was a terrible businessman and ended up going to jail for either murder or rape, she wasn't sure, that was ahead of her time but she knew what he did was really really bad, definitely something worthy of confession. Who knew when it was rescued—the wood scarred by stacks of bottles not to mention being antiqued with a wash of blue and brown paint in the seventies—*then* found by a young gay couple, who had meticulously restored it and for a generation used it as the center attraction of many cocktail parties. "I lied." "I cheated." "I coveted my neighbor's car . . ." " . . . house" ". . . wife." "*Forgive me.*"

The woman became more and more animated with her tales of hilarity, and they wondered after, while having coffee, how the woman knew all of those stories. Had she been a witness at one of the parties or was it all hearsay or imagined—a good story to move some merchandise? She had also spoken of Edwardian button hooks with a similar passion and Theodore Haviland and Limoges China of the 1920s, a nosegay pattern in pink and blue that she herself collected and loved but of course would certainly consider the right offer from an eager buyer, perhaps a young couple still searching for their pattern? "People don't always choose a pattern as they once did," she added, "but this will be a big regret of the generation, I'm certain." They didn't tell her that they, too, were part of the sleek Ikea culture she kept referencing and that the only antiques in their lives before this purchase were their parents, who only visited occasionally, because they were on the other coast.

She told them about a rocking chair thought to be haunted and how it would begin rocking slowly, creak by creak, when music was playing—but not just any music. The chair really liked a particular piece by Chopin; perhaps the spirit had once danced or had some kind of life-changing experience as the music played, though once she said she did hear it rocking to a commercial on television, a Hoover vacuum cleaner ad, something she has yet to understand. She had a Franciscan Desert Rose dessert plate that once held a piece of coconut cake eaten by Jackie Kennedy. The plate had never been washed, a dull dry smudge marring one side.

They left that day but couldn't stop thinking of the confessional and how wonderful it might look in their home. It would be the focal point, something they would talk about for the rest of their lives, a symbol of their marriage, and by the time they went to bed that night, they had decided they had to have it, in fact, they were filled with the awful anxiety that everyone who saw it would feel that way and so were there waiting when the woman arrived to unlock the door. She smiled knowingly as if to say I told you so, and gave them the number of a man who could deliver it.

The confessional looked even larger once it arrived; it filled their small living room and led to many jokes. He liked to refer

to the holy trinity of I, Myself, and Me. *Eat, Drink*, he com-
manded, sometimes sounding Biblical but more often like an
R-rated version of *Alice in Wonderland*. He would grab and pull
her in close for a hard kiss. *Eat. Drink. I want your money and
I want your time.*

A friend or semifriend—they weren't really crazy about him
even though he was always included—had once been an altar
boy and, inspired by Tom Waits's version of the song of that
name, made up his own verses in hopes of a laugh which is what
he was always doing, sometimes annoyingly, going for a laugh.
"Little altar boy, keep your back against the wall. Little altar
boy, don't answer if you get the call."

The friend's date, a quiet, serious woman getting her PhD
in history said she was tired of his jokes and that it all made
her really uncomfortable—the whole scene made her uncomfortable—that it was disrespectful and also silly that the only
conversations kept getting stuck on that *monstrous piece of furniture* making a joke of anything serious. She hadn't meant for
them to hear her, but they did, and when she realized, she turned
bright red and soon excused herself right out of the party never
to be heard from again. Her date said, *good riddance*, and that
he'd now like to confess how he only asked her out because he
felt sorry for her and now more than ever. *What a loser*, he said
and began to tell personal things about her behavior in bed and
that she was a walking yeast infection who did a terrible job
managing money; he'd seen at least one overdue bill in her apartment and everything in her refrigerator was past expiration date.

Promise you will never do that to me, they said before going
to bed that night, horrified by all the details they now knew of

the quiet, timid girl who everyone had thought was too good to go out with their semifriend anyway.

But the games continued. There were confessions of little white lies, embarrassing moments from childhood and adolescence. Some nights, when it was just the two of them, each in their separate compartments, they leaned close and whispered their own: In high school he stole twenty dollars off his father's dresser and when he saw how easy it was, kept doing it. When his parents had company and left their coats and purses on the bed, he slipped in and helped himself to a few dollars here and a few dollars there, something he had still done around the holidays if a lot of people showed up. She had once taken some nail polish from CVS but felt so guilty she returned it to the shelf the next day even though she had opened it and used it, her pearly pink nails a reminder. Oh, and she was once responsible for feeding a neighbor's cat but forgot to do it. They had returned from Myrtle Beach, shocked to see how skinny Pearl looked and that there was no water left in the toilet bowl. *What on earth?* They cried. *Thank God we left the seat up!* They gave her the little monogrammed anklet they had bought in appreciation—what else could they do with her initials there in curly script—but they never asked for her help again. In fact, they never spoke to her again and a few others in the neighborhood followed suit.

"Oh, you were a poor, innocent child," he said from inside his side of the box, his voice deep and slow, as it always was when they were playing. She said that actually she was in her twenties but, yes, still childlike in many ways, and she was thrilled that he, unlike those hard-hearted neighbors, could forgive her. He got quiet, just the sound of his breath, and she could tell he was trying not to laugh when he told her what she had to do to be fully forgiven. And of course, it became sexual. So much easier in this anonymous way, not unlike the texts they had sent early in their relationship. They wanted to whisper, their words coated in incense and age, mouths near the dark screen saying things only fantasy would allow.

Some days one of them started laughing and they couldn't stop, but on others the time passed in dark dreamlike waves, late afternoon turning to night, and it was hard to look at one another after.

It seemed there was no end to the well of secrets. It was not her he'd come to see that night after they had broken up, but her friend across the hall. He had always really liked her friend and in fact, the two of them had gotten together one weekend, before the breakup, when she had gone to see her parents. He had thought he could get to the door without her seeing him, but *busted*. He said she was so glad to see him, how could he ever tell her the truth?

"Until now," she said. That would have been when her father was *dying*, and she almost said that. Instead she said: "I once read your journal." That was not really true, but his sharp intake of breath followed by silence let her know there was substance there, something to be learned.

SHE: Sometimes the way you chew gets on my last nerve and I have yet to see you floss.

HE: She meant nothing to me—I wanted to make you jealous—and now that you're ruining the game and saying mean things, if you read my journal, you ought to know that, and you also ought to know I hate when you spray your hair like an old woman. I hate when you eat in bed and wipe your hand on the sheet.

Truce—the rope momentarily placed down in the grass and abandoned like a snake that could rear its head at any time. And then . . .

HE: I once saw this kid running from a parent—I assumed a parent—in the parking lot of Home Depot. The man had a belt wrapped around his wrist and the kid called him a hateful son of a bitch and screamed for someone to help him. I didn't know what I was seeing. The guy looked decent enough except for that belt.

He wants her to say there was nothing he could have done about it, but she refuses to give him that so easily. She would have called 911, or if not that, she would have at least said something to the store manager. The silence grows uncomfortable and finally in her slow, measured priestess voice she says: You must never do that again.

HE: I swear I will never do that again. I will never do nothing if I see a kid running from a man with a belt in his hand in the Home Depot parking lot when the store is closed.

SHE: You didn't say the store was closed, her mind actively creating the movie: a boy, a belt, a scream for help in a dark, empty parking lot. Was this a sin of omission?

HE: Oh and I sold sperm at the sperm bank as often as they would let me and when I hit my quota, I used my roommate's ID and went back to sell more.

SHE: I detest how the women in your family have bouts of pain and upset and take to their beds like limp Southern idiots and people wonder where the stereotypes come from. I once put some random NoDoz in the aspirin bottle and replaced the ibuprofen on your mother's dresser with Correctol—same size, both pink. I thought she needed to be up and moving.

Silence behind the screen. Obviously, he did not see the humor. Perhaps he was even recalling his mother's jittery eyes and hands and many times being excused that particular Thanksgiving.

Whenever she confessed, it occurred to her that there were many people who used knowledge as power, something to remind and lord over their victims: *Poor you, remember how you did this and said that?* What if a priest or therapist lost their mind and spewed it all into the world, all the exhaled foul breath of a long-ago morning that was supposed to be caught and held there in the velvet fabric until the end of time? They had both seen humans take the edge when they could get it, like their semi-friend, spitting secrets and painful intimacies as soon as his date walked out and no one listening could make eye contact, which, they decided, is where the idea of a confessional—the lack of visible contact—might have originated in the first place.

HE: I once sat outside of a grocery store at the beach wearing sunglasses and carrying a cane. Got enough money for a tank of gas and six-pack of beer.

SHE: I once stuck a tiny needle in and out of my brother's condom packs.

She loved his girlfriend and assumed this would ensure that she would be her sister-in-law and in her life forevermore. Who could have known that the girl would keep the problem all to herself, that she would panic and seek some backward avenue, to terrible results.

No one ever found out.

HE: When I had a summer job at US Air, I routinely stole little things from bags. Keys or parking tickets—the kinds of things people would assume they left behind.

He said he had a whole collection of these items and she thought how that explained all that shit—not just keys and parking tickets—in the lockbox at the back of his closet. Easy to pick the lock, strange things to have taken.

"You've stolen an awful lot," she said later, when they were eating dinner. This was breaking the rule they had agreed on: *All that is confessed stays inside the box.* "You're quite the seasoned thief."

"Well, you're a liar," he said. "And a rule breaker!" He said he would grant absolution when the time was right.

HE: There was a kid in my junior high forced to do things in the bathroom at lunch. Do things. I guarded the door so my friend didn't get caught. His friend.

She listened in silence as he told the details—one boy grew up and hit it big, a real star, and no one knew what happened to the other, moved before graduation. *Who knows?* Who knows.

HE: And here's one I've never told, talk about comedy of errors. One summer when I was working in Colorado I faked testicular cancer to get a girl to sleep with me. I biked a lot then and this girl (the unnamed girl) seemed impressed by that so it was natural to let the parallels with Lance continue. Lance was still a hero, everybody wearing his wristbands in support, and I told her I couldn't help but notice how much she looked like Sheryl Crow. (Oh my God.) All I wanted to do was have some fun—remember that song?—all I wanted was one night, but next thing I knew she was raising money, and not for Lance to get her own wrist band, but for *me*. She raised like over a thousand dollars.

She listened, trying to picture this. She had never seen him ride a bike, had never heard him sing or hum that song. In all of his drawers and stashes, she had never seen a Livestrong bracelet.

Is that a sin? he asked. I mean I didn't intend for it to go that way.

After a long silence, she asked what he did with the money. After a long pause, he said that he bought a used car and left without telling anyone. Anything else to confess? she asked and he said, yes. He had one more and then he was pretty sure he would have told all the big ones.

HE: I once dated this woman who liked to get rough, you know? Rough? Well, yeah, you know, playing around the way some people do. A lot of people like it, right? So no judgment. I've taken a vow. Anyway, we thought we ought to have a safe word.

A safe word? All she could think in the moment was of a game she and her siblings had played as children. Someone farted or burped, and everyone had to say *safety* and lick one finger and touch something blue. Why? Last one to speak and touch blue lost. Someone always lost.

So, we broke up after a year or so and last I heard she was marrying this guy from California. That was years ago and then about a year ago I get this call and it's all muffled-sounding and then I hear her say the word. (She said the word? He didn't tell this?) And then what happened? I figured she dialed me by mistake or was just up to her old tricks. (Old tricks?!) She said the word and then the phone went dead.

"Oh my God," she said. "The woman needed help! What did you do and why didn't you tell me?"

"I didn't think it was important, or maybe I thought you'd be upset. I don't know."

"Did you call to check on her?"

"No, it wasn't her number. She was crazy, right? Like the wildest person I ever knew, and I didn't want anything to do with her." He got up and walked into the kitchen to mix a drink. "You broke the rules again, so let's quit."

"You always want to quit," she said. "You take your turn and then you want to quit. What was the safe word?"

"I can't even think. So did you have a big confession or something? Like did you slip my mother some acid or an ex-lax?"

"I was married before I met you," she said. "But I'll just wait for my turn. I'll wait for you to remember and finish your turn." She really was married but this didn't seem like the right time to talk about it. Perhaps there would never be a right time and besides, what did it matter? The poor guy was dead and she was acquitted. She was innocent, they said so.

"What? You were married and never told me?"

"No, I'm a liar, remember? My confession is that I used your toothbrush."

"That's it?? Like you used it in your mouth or to scrub the bathroom?"

"My mouth, just my mouth."

"Are you sure you weren't married before?"

"Yes. Are you sure you don't recall that word?"

"Yes. If I knew, I would confess."

Over time, the heavy, dark monstrosity lost its appeal. They had said all they had to say and it was no longer fun. Even their friends had grown tired of it; even the semifriend had run out of grotesque things to say, which everyone found was a relief. They had to get rid of it because there was no room for comfortable chairs if they were going to get the home-theater-sized television and host movie nights. When they told the strange little woman at the store, she nodded knowingly and then lifted her chin and stared up into the ceiling as if getting some message from the great beyond. She said she shouldn't be giving them such a good trade, but she would, and then led them to the perfect choice—an exquisite Victorian kissing chair from France. "The perfect tête-à-tête," she said and motioned to the ornately carved S-shaped chair, patted one of the velvet seats and beckoned them to sit, the polished wooden arm solid between them.

✳ The Last Station

Once a year, just as the dogwoods are about to come into bloom, Tori's mother straps a makeshift cross to her back and begins her trek across the front yard, stopping twelve times, just as Jesus had done over two thousand years before. She leaves out the last two stations, having never really incorporated *resurrection* into the show. With each stop, she shouts out various social injustices she has witnessed during the year. She was for a time artistic program director at the elementary school where she worked for thirty-five years as the librarian—elaborate productions of *Alice in Wonderland* and *The Wizard of Oz* to her credit—so of course she is aware of the dramatic and sometimes humorous effect her show has on those who stop and watch.

Tori's mother knows the power of comic relief and relies on it often when she is in danger of offending others. Politically, she leans left of center—not always a popular place to be in the Bible Belt—and yet she has managed to maintain a position of respect and authority in a very conservative town, even as people often talk behind her back or circle an index finger up to the head, whispering words like *nuts* and *sacrilegious*. Still, the majority chooses to overlook these things, because her success rate with the children who experienced her tutelage surpassed that of anyone else in the town's elementary school system. Children who were painfully shy learned to step forward with confidence, and those inclined to make trouble seemed to turn things around in ways that surprised even their parents. Tori knows that there was probably some bribing going on, because that's what she experienced all through childhood. "If you can learn the beginning to the Gettysburg Address and ask to recite it before your class, I will let you get a puppy." Tori's fourth grade teacher was a confirmed racist, and Tori's mother once led a statewide campaign to change the way people discussed the Civil War in classrooms, begging that people stop saying "We lost" because "There are a lot of *us* who don't want to be included in the *we*."

"Are you bribing her again?" Tori's dad had called from the next room. He reminded her how, just the year before, she had bought Tori an Astronaut Barbie for playing with the kid everybody in the neighborhood made fun of because her ears stuck out and she came from somewhere in the Midwest where people drank *pop*.

"Positive reinforcement," Tori recalled her mother saying. "It might look like a bribe but when it is for doing the right thing, then it is just positive reinforcement." Tori never told how that new girl said everybody in the neighborhood was stupid and how Tori's dad must not be very successful if Tori's mom had to work all the time. She told Tori ("No offense, but . . .") she really didn't want anybody to see her playing over there in Loserville.

In the beginning, Tori's mother's walks were all about what she felt was best for the children of the town, the state, the country, the world. She wrote a piece for the local paper that got picked up and reprinted across the state: SACRIFICING OUR KIDS—ANYONE FOR RESURRECTION? She was outraged that theirs was a state where physical punishment was still allowed, that pre-K programs had been cut down to nothing, and that they were threatening to take away the free breakfast offered to those kids who arrived at school with empty stomachs and pockets. "Hello?" Tori's mother liked to call out to the audience, "This is in the Bible, folks. Jesus said he was hungry and no one fed him. He knocked on that door and no one answered." She had repeated the monologue only a year ago, Tori's dad still very much alive. "All you have to do is turn the knob."

"And," Tori's Uncle Sanford called from the edge of the yard, where he was eating a plate of food from their kitchen and drinking one of Tori's dad's beers, "does anybody remember that song that went: 'I hear you knocking but you can't come in'?" He took a long swallow and nudged Tori's dad into laughter. "Did that song come from the Bible, you guess?"

Tori's mother ignored Sanford, as she often did, and continued saying that by choosing not to vaccinate their children, a small percentage of people had compromised and thrust everyone backward. Guns? Don't even get her started. Her calm storytelling voice grew louder as she made her way across the yard, each station a little more dramatic as she put forward the plea that people pay more attention to their children. "They will be in charge of you some day," she liked to say. "We're all going to get old and die, right?" she would ask the quiet crowd.

But then she always knew just when to turn the tide to something most everyone could embrace, expanding her attention to local news stories or what she saw as unfortunate fashion choices. How could they as a community work to have the starlings lured away from the courthouse trees to those along the river so cars and unlucky passersby didn't get covered in droppings? How could they persuade people not to hover and spray the toilet seats in the Porta Johns set up for the Little League games? Convince people to scoop up after their dogs?

"Sounds like this is an elimination process you're focused on," Sanford said.

"Are folks as tired of reality television as I am? And of people being famous just because they were born rich?" She looked around for affirmation. "Let the poncho return, but for God's sake don't reclaim the wide tie or leisure suit. Jumpsuits! Who said they could come back? And who gives a damn about keeping up with the Kardashians or those who had all of those children without ever kissing or holding hands?"

As well as her Stations Show, Tori's mother does a popular Halloween reading of local ghost stories and a feminist Christmas event highlighting Mrs. Claus and all that she did to keep things on schedule. "You think he exercises?" she would ask the children. "You think he's gluten-free?" She once even held a barbecue for the neighborhood dogs and had thirty or more sitting and waiting for hot dogs.

Tori admires her mother and the many stands she takes, but
it hasn't been easy to be her daughter, especially in childhood
and adolescence when she was regularly asked by other children,
Is she really your mother? and it was confusing as to whether
it was a compliment or an insult. Tori had dreaded years in the
carpool line when she had to get into her mother's car, the whole
back end covered in bumper stickers proclaiming her various
beliefs. Even now, as this year's Stations gets underway, her fear
of embarrassment leaves her standing off to the side to watch.

A lot has happened over the past year, and at times Tori
had wondered if her mother would perform at all. Her father
had a stroke only days after Tori's mother retired from the public school system, just weeks after last year's iteration of this
very performance, where he had watched from the crowd with
Sanford. After the stroke, he lived three months without being
able to speak. During that time, Tori's mother had sat by his side
vigilantly, telling him that he was going to get better, repeating
back all the plans they had made over the years. She kept a pad
and pen and kept extending it, wanting him to write something,
but he usually just stared back blankly or wrote what he wanted
to eat. She leaned in close and sang his favorite songs, read to
him, and then he died the one afternoon she went to get her hair
cut. "Why?" she had asked. "Why? What about that hot tub
he said we might get? What about 'I love you' or 'Good-bye'?"

The idea to lug a cross from one corner of the front yard to
the other stemmed from a town-wide interdenominational move-
ment called Walk the Walk where, in preparation for Easter,
kids were encouraged to carry a two-foot cross wherever they
went for a week. It was designed to sound hip and exciting, to

pull kids away from the dark recesses of their video arcades and back seats and basements, to get them to put down their Frisbees and skateboards and joints and follow along. The crosses were made of Styrofoam so children wouldn't worry about splinters or muscle strain. Tori's mother said she thought that defeated the purpose; however, she didn't dismiss the idea as she normally would have because Tori, then in junior high school, had been invited by a much more popular girl to participate.

"Do you want to do that, Tori?" her mother had asked. They were in the backyard watching Tori's dad light the charcoal. They did this every Saturday night and had for as long as Tori could remember: chicken kabobs on the grill, baked potatoes and garlic bread, her mother's lemon chess pie, flowers on the table. It was important to Tori's mother, and she said the same things each week: *Aren't the flowers beautiful?* and *Isn't it a lovely night?* She said this even on cold, rainy nights when they ate in the kitchen under fluorescent lighting. Uncle Sanford always came over, rain or shine, but that night the weather was pleasant, springlike. "It might be fun, honey," her mother said.

It was obvious that she was desperate for something, *anything*, to happen that might open up Tori's social life. Her mother was not an avid churchgoer; in fact, she had routinely complained to the principal when visitors began or ended a program with prayer, particularly when they ended with references to Jesus or to the Father, Son, and Holy Ghost. She spoke often of separation of church and state. She designated herself as representative for Sam Berkowitz, the only Jew at the elementary school, and Mahmud Thompson, whose mother's parents had just moved from India. *Red and yellow, black and white*, she was known to say when anyone tried to argue her points, spouting back to them the childhood hymn that proclaimed Jesus's love for everyone.

But because the invitation had come from Elizabeth and promised that Tori might be included in other invitations as well, Tori's mother was there 100 percent, encouraging her to read about all the different faiths and what each offered. Elizabeth and several others in Tori's class were Baptists and went to a sunrise revival every spring where they ate doughnuts and cupcakes first thing in the morning and then all rode the bus together, exiting in front of the junior high like a flock of overfed sheep. Tori wanted camaraderie, that was all, and she also liked Elizabeth's older brother, a long-haired boy who played the drums in a band and who had, she heard, won a bet on that revival bus by eating a dozen doughnuts in less than five minutes.

The fact that Tori's mother was trying to convince her to get out and Walk the Walk meant that even her mother saw her social placement at the junior high school in a desperate place. "If nothing else, you'll meet people, or see someone you've always known in a different, brand-new light." She glanced over at Tori's dad when she said this. He was healthy then—tall and tan, weekends spent fishing or sitting in the backyard whittling the various toys he made in his spare time. "It's good to be attentive to others," she continued, a little louder. "Right, Ed? *Attentive?*"

"Huh?" he asked, and it was unclear to Tori if his response was real or a joke. Her father was an electrician who often said things like *Let there be light!* or *Shocking!* or *Watt's new, pussycat?* He was very good with his hands and had a whole collection of thin strips of wire of all different colors, which he used to connect the wooden train cars he carved or to tie sails to the tiny boats he made, to put antennae on little pipe-cleaner caterpillars. He once made Tori a dollhouse and wired it so that every room had lamps that really worked.

Walk the Walk began the same year Tori's mother took an interest in sewing and made all of her own clothes; she was standing there in what looked like a large lavender pillowcase, a self-created style she thought would look good on Tori, too. It was not lost on Tori—a good twenty pounds heavier than she should have been—that this was her mother's way of trying to address her appearance, as if Tori herself didn't want to look and feel better. Still, she had enough sense to know that wearing a purple pillowcase to junior high was *not* going to help.

"It's important to explore and figure out who you are." Her mother opened her eyes wide, and her dad did that thing where he pretended to stick his finger in a socket and get electrocuted.

"Tell us who *you* are then," Uncle Sanford said. "A nut job? A purple people eater?"

Uncle Sanford was not bad-looking at all and often had dates in the early years, back when he was still young enough for women blessed with a streak of optimism to think he might get his act together and make good on one of his many business ideas he swore would take him from his position at Home Depot in lawn and garden to a home office someplace like Hilton Head where he wouldn't really have to work at all. He had nearly died in a motorcycle crash in his late twenties, and so everyone cut him a lot of slack, especially Tori's dad, who laughed at all of his jokes and gave enthusiastic support to each and every farfetched idea. People said there had been damage in the crash—a kind of arrested development—and gave this as the reason he had continued to date girls in their early twenties until it got really creepy. Tori's mother had once argued that the accident was a convenient alibi, that Sanford had always been a little off and he had always talked that slow, with more pauses and long sighs than was bearable. She said that the crash had allowed the whole family to look away from genetics and blame a sharp turn on a gravel road instead. By the time he was forty, the twenty-year-olds who went out with him *really* had problems. He said, "That dress is ugly. Most girls want to look sexy."

"What do *you* know about women or their clothes?" Tori's mother asked. "You've never even had a steady girl."

"That may be," Sanford said and straightened up. "But I have had a wobbly one or two."

Tori's father thought that was very funny. He laughed and pulled Tori's mother in close as if he could push his loyalty to Sanford into her. "Forgive him, for he knows not what he does."

Tori's mother liked to say things like *Be the change you want to see* and *Seize the day*. She was saying *We can do it* with her arm muscle in view before Rosie the Riviter came back into fashion. She nudged Tori into accepting the invitation to pick up her Styrofoam cross and Walk the Walk with Elizabeth, even though Tori feared it might be very similar to the year before, when she was invited to proselytize in the Burger King and outside of Dairy Joy, which proved humiliating to say the least. The church youth director had coached them to ask lots of questions (*Are you saved?*) and then planted himself with a Whopper in the far corner to watch and take notes about who was doing a good job. He tried to look young by wearing lots of turquoise and unbuttoning his shirt but no one was fooled. One necklace in particular made his round, Charlie Brown head look like a balloon tied off and about to pop. Tori got through it all by politely stepping up, brochures in hand, and asking, "Could I get you some ketchup or mustard or extra napkins?" People looked at her like she was strange but many said yes and so this took up a lot of time. She told the people she was waiting on that this was a new service Burger King was trying out and she told the youth director that everyone she spoke to was already saved and attending church regularly elsewhere but really appreciated her concern. Tori was a pleaser, the kiss of death. She explained her resistance to the idea of walking the Walk, even as much as she wanted to be a part of the group, but her mother said she had nothing to lose. Her mother also said that she was thinking about doing her own version of Walk the Walk. "Wouldn't that be something?" she asked and smiled, leaving them all to wonder.

That was fifteen years ago, and now, Tori is married and lives two hours away. During this time, her mother has perfected the Stations Show, stopping for longer periods of time, her notions of what merits a shout-out growing by leaps and bounds. When she neared retirement and no longer feared an early dismissal from the school board should people complain about her, it all got turned up a notch. Anything she witnesses—a cross word, someone breaking in line, people in nursing homes drugged into comas, a person failing to say "Thank you" or open a door for someone who needs help, saying "No prob" instead of "You're welcome," a drive-by shooting, young people not bothered at all about showing their cracks, more guns than people—she has recorded and saved up for this proclamation, a sheet from a legal pad with her tiny scrawl clutched in one hand.

For all her vehemence, she has yet to discuss her sadness over Tori's father's death. If Tori mentions the cemetery or what her dad might have liked, her mother launches into a rant over something she perceives to be unjust. "And there is a lot of injustice!" she said this morning while getting ready. "So much unexplained injustice!"

Fifteen years ago, neighbors peeped out of their windows, but now there is a regular community following, people gathering and lining the street in front of the house where Tori grew up—a brick ranch at the end of a cul-de-sac, a thick row of evergreens hiding the interstate, where the sound of trucks and cars rises and falls like the ocean—as soon as Tori's mother comes out into the yard and pulls her cross from the garage. This year two towheads recently transplanted from upstate New York have set up a lemonade stand and are raking in the profits. They argue over the taste and how to make change. The older boy, his Yankees cap perched off to one side, tells his little brother that if there's no change to give back, people will just give you the whole dollar. Tori's mother studies his cap. She never allowed that look in the school library; she says it makes children look simpleminded, like their jaws should be hanging slack like a drawbridge over an empty creek. She takes a pen from behind her ear and makes a note.

The performance begins. She reads from police blotters, lengthy lists of charges for child abuse and neglect. She cites the Proud Boys and enumerates an ever-growing number of hate crimes. Her book club never goes with her selection but opts for things she thinks are stupid! People got mad at her this past Christmas for trying to boycott Elf on the Shelf, for fear of instilling paranoia in young, imaginative minds. But what else is going to happen if you tell someone he is under constant surveillance? She falls once, gets up. Her breath is labored.

In the time since that first performance, which brought *no* new friends Tori's way (her mother said they just weren't smart enough to appreciate a girl like her), Tori graduated third in her class, took up Pilates, and lost twenty pounds. She earned a degree in history and then her PhD and now teaches at the university. She also met William, fell head over heels in love with him and married quickly. William is the kind of handsome that Tori is sure leaves people wondering why he is with her. He's tall and has not an ounce of body fat, a natural athlete who loves to play golf and has promised that they will visit every major golf course in their life together. *Is that what you want, Tori?* she imagines her mother asking. *Is that what you want?*

William majored in philosophy—his mother told Tori he had always liked to argue—and then went to medical school; the first time she brought him home, he talked about his cadaver, Stu, like he was a good friend, while Tori's dad talked about a program he'd seen about a Ping-Pong champion, and then they both started talking golf. It was like they were playing Ping-Pong themselves, taking turns talking but not really ever listening—Taiwan, slam, ipsilateral, bogey, ventral, poor Stu, backspin, par—with Sanford occasionally piping in about how he was almost a geologist but couldn't get his rocks off; he was almost a lawyer but lost his briefs and couldn't pass a bar; he was going to be a doctor but had no patience.

But William had asked her out and then he had asked her out again, this man who was the grown-up version of all those boys who had looked right through Tori on their way to games and parties, and then in college, fraternity parties and debutante balls. The khaki-clad, madras bow-tied, sockless loafer boys who danced well, and it didn't really matter if they made good grades or not because they would still land on their feet. Sometimes she still wonders what he saw in her. "You are beautiful, Tori," her mother told her on her wedding day. "Inside and out, and don't you ever forget it." Tori's mother had worn a dress she would never have normally picked: a traditional navy linen with plain navy pumps and conventional gold knot earrings. Tori assumed she had bought it for this occasion and likely would never wear it again. It was almost as if her mother had asked herself: *What would make Tori feel most comfortable when I meet William's family?* And then, remarkably, she did it.

"Forty years of marriage and thirty-five years working in the library! Thirty-five years at the elementary school, and all I got was a lamp. A lamp! And I don't even like it. It's all colonial like it ought to be in a museum in Williamsburg, VA! I'm afraid if I rub it somebody like Paul Revere will pop out. I love modern-looking things but who knew? Who cares? I wanted to live in a modern-looking house, but your dad said he would feel like he was part of an ant farm. But, I *wanted* that. Why didn't I get to *want* something? A lamp. That is what all those years of my life are worth!"

"Mom, please." Tori made the drive today, fearing something like this might happen.

Her mother is hunched forward for dramatic effect. She is wearing black stretch shorts that hit just above her knee and an oversize pink T-shirt and white Keds. Her hair has already drooped in the humidity of the late afternoon, coarse gray bangs plastered to her forehead.

"Children came to me and said, 'I want *Charlotte's Web*,' and I gave them what they wanted! I shushed those who wanted to tell what was going to happen and ruin it for everybody. A child bit my hand and I clenched my teeth and let him, all to keep him from revealing Charlotte's sad death to the big-eyed little girl who had entered that world and was clinging, for her very daily salvation, to that fine filamented web."

She turns now and faces her audience, staring at the new couple from across the street—their boys the ones with the lemonade stand—and waits for them to make eye contact. "How many of us can identify with Charlotte? Raise your hand! Who can identify with working your ass off, toiling through the night at some task so some pig, sweet though he may be, can slop around in the mud and have himself a high old time?" Several people laugh nervously and raise their hands. A woman asks if this is part of the show, she had heard it was funny and this doesn't seem funny.

"*But Charlotte loves Wilbur!*" Tori says. "She *loves* him."

Tori's mother stops and looks at her. She had recently asked if Tori was happy in her marriage. What did the two of them do together? What did they have in common? What did they talk about? What did William do or say that let Tori know how important she was in his life? How did she know for sure that William was really at work all those late hours? And her question had left Tori wondering things she had never thought to wonder. Just the other day, she found herself pulling his clothes from the hamper and sniffing like a dog for signs of another life out there. She felt self-conscious at night when she undressed for bed, not wanting him to see the lines and dimples of her previous weight. He hadn't really said anything, but he didn't have to; it was the way he looked at her if she ate a cookie or bowl of ice cream or stretched out to take a nap in the middle of the day. She once even caught him looking at the Fitbit he had given her for Christmas to read the step count. Now she often hooks it to their neighbor's retriever's collar and then spends a good hour or so tossing a stick while sitting in the sun; William has also commented on how white she is. Tori loves to watch the big black dog running back and forth and back and forth. One day she had over twenty-five thousand steps and so she was sure to leave the Fitbit on the coffee table where William would see it. Lately it has been so hard to shake the realization that he never would have looked at her twice as a younger woman; he would have looked right through her. And *was* she happy?

"Behold, your mother!" She spreads her arms wide, the cross quivering in her hand. "My birthday came and went and no one remembered. I forgave your dad. I blamed his stroke. He spent a lot of time those last days staring at old photos—not of us that I ever saw, but of himself, maybe with a friend or two, sturdy on two legs with a fish or a baseball bat or bowling ball. Man's man. All decked out like Elmer Fudd and grinning like a Cheshire cat and holding whatever there'd been to catch—fish, hog, football. He was almost completely paralyzed, so no, of course he didn't run out and get a gift but still, if he could gesture for food or drink for me to fetch like a dog, why couldn't he do 'Happy Birthday'?" She pauses, breathing hard, her face flaming.

A little girl in a pink sundress says she looks like Ursula in *The Little Mermaid* and hides behind her mother, crying. The child's mother is someone Tori recognizes from high school, someone always cheerful and pleasant, but who, now that Tori's mother is clearly crossing into a bad place, has stopped making eye contact and is slowly backing away toward her car. "I was told this was like a play," the woman says to the man beside her, perhaps wanting to be heard. "I heard that she was great with kids."

"For thirty-five years!" Tori's mother screams. "I was great with the kids for thirty-five years! And what's it worth? A lamp! A dumb-watted, dim-witted lamp! A woman who lived forty years with an electrician isn't excited about a lamp!"

She points at Tori and breathes heavily, nostrils flared like a bull about to charge. "And what was your excuse?"

Tori jumps at the sudden attention, her mother frozen, cross held forward and aimed at Tori like a weapon. She feels the eyes of the neighborhood as her mother waits.

"All day I waited for a call." And down she goes, the cross by her side. Tori *had* forgotten her mother's birthday. It was one of those days caught up in her own indecision and worries; she had gone to an award ceremony honoring one of her students and she was being reviewed for tenure. That day William didn't like the color she had painted the dining room or the color of her toenails; William doesn't like a lot of things—even his mother has told her that about him—and Tori has begun wearing clothes she never would have chosen for herself, loud colors and little waist-cinching belts; she longs for her mother's pillowcase muu-muu style. Tori missed the birthday and she misses her dad and now she's missed her period, and has the sick feeling she has missed her chance in life. Now she can't find words beyond *I'm sorry*.

"Sometimes I felt so unloved," Tori's mother says, her voice lowering to a whisper. "Invisible and unloved."

"But he did love you," Tori says. "Dad always loved you. And I love you."

Tori's mother leans the cross against the trunk of a pine tree and presses her forehead into it. "You had beautiful birthdays," she whispers and then she gets louder, like a volume knob suddenly turned. "Chocolate—and sweat-stained children running all over the house and yard and smearing hands on my walls and the sofa I couldn't afford to replace. Can you even imagine that? And you had a beautiful wedding, Tori. Do you remember that? I gave up broccoli because Ed hated the taste. Gave up having cats because Ed hated the smell. I never went on a fancy vacation because Ed hated to fly. I had to be the disciplinarian! I have only had two pedicures in my entire life, but I've paid for you to have about two thousand. Why? Why do we do these things?"

"I thought you were a disciple." Sanford, who has been watching from the curb, looks over at one of the young mothers who is politely trying not to engage with him, then looks back at Tori's mom. "Oh, I see," he says, his voice getting louder. "You're pretending you *are* Jesus. So, like, aren't you supposed to *give* the pedicures?"

Tori's mother glares at Sanford but doesn't speak, then squats and puts her head between her knees like she might faint. Tori's father had had three strokes in all, and Sanford, trying to be poetic at the funeral, had said his brother's life was like a baseball game—Tori's dad was a man who had barely rounded second base, a man completely in the game, and then, "Stroke one and stroke two and stroke three." It did not go over well, but people were polite because it was Sanford and because everyone had heard about his accident years before. People also did not want to be included on Tori's mother's list for the upcoming production.

"Is she okay?" someone asks, and in a faint voice Tori's mother says that she's thirsty. One of the towheaded children is forced by his mother to give her a Dixie cup of lemonade. She stares up at him, his cap off to one side the way she hates, and Tori holds her breath for what is to come, but her mother just takes the small cup and nods her thank you, then ignores when the child says she owes him fifty cents. "I thirst. I promised some scripture. There's a little scripture."

"You get more and more theatrical, Mom." Tori says, desperate to snap her out of this, desperate to lighten the mood and for the show to end. "Please, let's call it a day."

"But I'm not finished," she says, her voice nearly as slow as Sanford's. "When it is finished, I will say, 'It is finished.' Meanwhile, I have other things to say, things like how I feel I have sacrificed myself without even asking why. Without asking those I was sacrificing *for* if it even mattered. Maybe it never mattered. Even Mother Teresa got frustrated, and who in the hell could blame her? We all need reassurance, don't we? We need booster shots, right? Why should we think that one little promise at one little altar when you're not old enough to know better is enough for a lifetime?"

Tori hears a neighbor ask if she should call a doctor or the police or something. Her mother stands and spins around with the cross before heading off in a new direction. Someone else says it was a good thing she no longer worked at the school. *Looney Tunes. Meshugeneh. Certified.*

Tori's mother looks up into the trees and continues. "What if all that we believe is just another story? A good ghost story? A good, heartfelt haunting."

People are leaving. Those who remain are watching with looks of great sadness, arms hanging in that impotent way reserved for when they don't know what to do. "The only one who ever seemed to notice what was going on with me was Dolly."

Tori winces with the accusation but also smiles at the thought of Dolly, her mother's constant companion for years, a sweet yellow pudding of a dog. Before she can speak to say she is sorry, her mother continues. "Sometimes I thought your father liked being with his buddies more than he liked being with me. My ideas held nothing for him, my books or programs on television, my ideas about what might be fun. I'd say, 'Let's watch a movie, Ed.' 'Let's sit here and watch the sun go down.'"

Sanford counts out fifty pennies to the towheaded children from New York, and now the four-foot entrepreneur is pissed off as he has to make change for the next customer. He points to Tori's mother and tells Sanford somebody has to pay for her lemonade.

"Ed said I needed to find a group to be with. I think he was tired of me wanting to spend time with him, but was I wrong to want his attention? Was I wrong to want all that he had prom-ised me in the beginning?"

Tori's mother pushes herself up, her face contorted like she might cry, and Tori hears someone telling another how usually it *is* funny, not like this at all, and Tori steps forward to where her mother is still sitting, red-faced and breathless. "Mom, please."

"All those years when so many mothers were staying home and baking cookies, I was working and feeling guilty that I wasn't at home and then when I saw that I could finally stay at home, so many women I knew and had envied were saying they were unfulfilled and picking up little jobs here and there or going back to school. And then your father dies and here I am. I have never been on the right path at the right time."

"Mom, *please.*"

"'Find some friends,' he said, so I joined that book club, remember? And what did we read but *Fifty Shades of Stupid.* What woman wants to be tied up and mistreated? Isn't that what has gone on and on forever? What were the damn sixties all about? Why in the hell would a smart woman want to be abused by some idiot? Why did I march and carry signs for the ERA? I'm a librarian for godsakes!"

"There was a time when you would have taken up for the sexually expressive," Sanford says. "And you would've done all your crap about why stupid books have rights, too." Sanford keeps waiting for a response but she ignores him, instead turn-ing to Tori.

"I didn't fit in except there in the library with a bunch of eight- and nine-year-olds. I didn't even fit in at home and your dad didn't notice. He had his buddies for fishing or golf or whatever and was fine not having a life with me," she whispers, the toe of her unlaced Ked pushing the cross away from her. "That's why I wanted you to make friends and find things you loved."

"Are you saying you think Ed was queer?" Sanford asks. He says it like it rhymes with *car.*

"Queer might've been easier. How do you explain *nothing*? I wanted us to talk about our life—break the bread, drink the wine. 'I had a wonderful day, dear, tell me about yours,' or 'I am so glad to be home because my day was terrible.' I wanted to tell him about the kids I knew, the boy who got upset while listening to *The Cat in the Hat* because he said his daddy would beat the snot out of him if he let the cat inside their house. Or the girl who kept a collection of paper clips she gave names to and kept in her pocket or the child who never spoke above a whisper and was afraid of loud sounds. Those I made it my business to help if needed—a toothbrush or comb, socks, lunch money—because they came and went out of neglect."

"I wanted to talk about you, Tori, and what you were doing in school, how I worried about how self-conscious you were, and then how you got too thin and how I had doubts about William, something not quite right about the way he treated you, but I knew better than to interfere and risk losing you."

"What?" Tori asks now. "What didn't you tell me?"

"I wanted to cry sometimes, but there was so little time to cry, and your father would say, 'Oh, you worry over nothing,' or 'I hate when you tell sad stories,' or 'What do you really have to complain about? Good job, retirement coming, nice house paid for, a daughter grown and married well. Dolly was just a dog.

Just a dog.'" She wipes her cheeks with the backs of her hands,
shakes her head in disbelief. "'Just a dog.'"

"Don't forget a handsome brother-in-law," Sanford pipes up,
but all the anger has left her and she just stares at him. Now her
mouth opens in a silent cry, and in that moment Tori sees years
of those hands fixing sandwiches or peeling potatoes or folding
laundry. Her mother drove that beat-up Honda for years, vol-
unteered at the soup kitchen and then returned to cook supper,
sometimes too exhausted, once in her red flannel nightshirt and
soft fuzzy socks, to even doze in front of an episode of *Murder,
She Wrote*. Her days were spent herding little flocks of children
in and out of the school library, giving dramatic readings and
inviting them to join her. New dresses were rare, the Saturday
night dinner the pot of gold at the end of each week. Tori thinks
of all the Christmases when Sanford sat with gifts around his
feet, his gift to her something from the remnant table, if he gave
her anything at all. Her mother faithfully bought gifts for everyone, including those children in need whose names and ages
appeared on the tree at the mall.

"And my birthday!" Tori's mother rolls to her side, tight
shorts straining at the seams, one bulging vein like a blue earth-
worm throbbing up the back of her left leg. "Even the next day I
waited! The belateds never came. I thought surely you all would
remember with the next time I sent you a card, but you just
cashed that check and went on. I was *forsaken!*" She picks herself up from the ground, her face reddened and slick with sweat.
"Yes, I felt sorry for myself, because how many times did I go to
Dainty Mae's bakery and pick up beautiful cakes, roses made of
icing, ballerinas for you and cowboys for Sanford?" She points

now to where he's standing. "I have treated him like my own brother or son all these years, and what's in it for me? A bunch of shitty dead plants from Home Depot that nobody wants."

"I thought you wanted resurrection," Sanford says. "'Tis the season. And those cakes you bought were sexist."

"Well, it didn't stop you from eating them, Great Oz of Home Depot. Ed said, 'Be nice to my brother, he's had a hard time.' 'I am my brother's keeper.' 'He ain't heavy, he's my brother,' and whatever other brother bullshit you can think of, and I said, 'Of course, honey, of course. Of course, Sanford is welcome in our home. Welcome to our food and our attention and our money and sympathy.' Here's my life, Sanford, take it. Here's paradise, eat it up." She lowers the cross and her chest heaves to get a breath like she might start sobbing any minute. For the first time Tori has ever witnessed, Sanford looks away and says nothing. "Ed had some kind of survivor's guilt about you. I guess he felt responsible for you his whole life. He always put you first, Sanford, even before your accident, so enjoy it!"

"Oh, Mom. Dad loved you." Tori says, feeling desperate. "He did." Her whole body feels different, and she knows her suspicions are correct, something she can't even bear to think about. *But what do you want, Tori?* her mother would ask. *What do you want, dear?*

"I was cheerful, wasn't I? Generous? But of course I wanted things." She moves to a new spot on the lawn, an area now in full shade. "And this is where Jesus would have promised his kingdom to the thief; it would be like if I promised everything to Sanford," she pauses, waits to get his attention. "For years I told myself that this was just my station in life. Oh, there were nights when he tried to tell me all that was in our future, nights when he made promises of how it all would be, what my grandmother would have called 'night talk'—like at revival, everybody getting saved and high on goodwill to man; like summer camp when you pledge your love and devotion even though you forget them as soon as you say good-bye to rusty lake water and s'mores and whatever else crap they fed you."

"Mama?" Tori steps forward. The sun is setting, and faint streaks of light soften her mother's face. "Mom, please. Let's go."

"But listen," her mother grabs her arm and holds on to it. "Life is short. And don't you guess Jesus hoped, right up to the last second, that someone would step in and *do something?*" She shakes her head, dark eyes swimming. "That someone would say, 'Oh honey, I'm so sorry. You don't deserve this.'" She squeezes Tori's arm harder, her hand shaking. "I want more. I want *my* turn and yet, here I am and it's all over—*finished.*" She breathes in a long, ragged breath, and Tori is trying to think of the right thing to say but before she can, her mother turns her head and studies Tori's face, as if trying to memorize every pore. "I'm betting Mother Teresa might've loved a pedicure." She stares up into the sky and closes her eyes. Even Sanford has left now, slumped forward in that way he always does when he wants someone to feel sorry for him. And Tori is sure that her mother will probably reach out to him to smooth things over before tomorrow arrives. But now, the last car door slamming, engines cranked and gone, Tori's mother laughs. Is she picturing Mother Teresa at a spa? Imagining what she will say to Sanford?

Sometime soon Tori will ask her mother what she was think-ing in that moment and she will ask what it was she saw in

William that worried her; she will ask her opinion about a lot of things, too many to even think about, and she will thank her for being there all those years Tori's clothes didn't fit quite right and she had trouble making friends. There's so much she wants to tell her, but for now she doesn't want to break the silence, her mother's hand cupping her own. For now, it is enough just to be here with her, shadows filling the yard. The only person left is the little blond boy in the crooked cap who is determined to get his lemonade money. His pockets jingle as he walks across the yard, and Tori watches her mother dig a ten-dollar bill from her back pocket and wave it high in the air. "Keep the change," she says when the child steps close to grab it, and then she stretches out in the cool, shaded grass, arms spread wide, ankles crossed.

✳ Act III

It's been years since they were all together for more than a holiday gathering, and over twenty years since they were in this place—mountain lake, paddleboats, hikes with bagged lunches. When Vera made the reservation, she told Glen that she had only one reason in mind, a gathering of their children—*because it all goes too fast*, she said—and now they are all there, arriving from their various adult lives and sliding right back into their childhood roles. William, the oldest, with his new wife, Maura, and her son, Eli; Suzanne (the one they had always thought would divorce) and her husband, Pete, with their toddler twins, Dakota and Jackie, who are only silent when deep in sleep; and last but never least, Rosie, the baby, and Derek, who she's madly in love with, perhaps the last in a long string of prospects that Glen said made him feel like he needed to hide his wallet. Rosie has a son, Tad, who is seven, and ready to record and repeat anything said. Glen called him TeleTad, and though they both felt guilty, they had done nothing to stop him the day he talked about visiting his daddy—Rosie's ex—who had become a preacher of "liberty skates" (*What the hell?* Glen asked) and wore a bathrobe like Jesus. "Wow," Vera said, "what does all that mean exactly, honey?" and Tad shrugged and went back to unscrewing every Oreo in the bag.

After years of teaching high school drama, nothing has yet to compare to the family encounters that have come and gone over the years, the children rotating under the spotlight with great regularity: weddings, births, jobs, William's divorce and remarry, a breakdown of sorts (Rosie after the soon-to-be *preacher* skipped town and she and Tad moved in for awhile), Suzanne and Pete taking turns with their many different degree pursuits. When Vera thinks of the first time they were here as a young family, it seems so simple.

The hotel is up in the mountains, a large turn-of-the-century wooden structure with a wraparound porch facing the lake. It was a croquet-on-the-lawn kind of place and it would not surprise her to turn and see men in striped coats and suspenders there in the gazebo singing something like "Bicycle Built for Two," a song that always made Vera laugh with the memory of her mother at the end of life in nursing care, complaining that that's the only song they sang other than depressing hymns that left everyone weeping and reminded they had one foot in the grave. She said when she closed her eyes at night after one of those sing-alongs, all she could see was Jesus on a bicycle. Vera's mother had lived way past her *expiration date*—her phrase, like life was nothing more than a quart of milk. "One day you'll know what I mean," she had said, the words garbled behind parched lips. And isn't that the all-occasion parental phrase?—*one day you'll know what I mean*—one that springs to Vera's mind often these days.

Vera had often instructed students in the importance of what haunts a scene, and now feels she has taken on the role herself. She has almost confided to Glen several times, but it has yet to be the right time. Why add to the burden of a difficult day? He comes home from work, tired and frustrated—are we ever where we intended to be? And likewise, why ruin a good day, the one where he feels accomplished, healthy, and seems more like himself. So many roles and so little time. Is there ever a right time?

It's like *The Shining*, Glen had said when they first came years ago. *Boats and bikers, croquet and hikers, and here's Johnny!* He was working hard in those days, part of the HR team at the community college, and he really didn't like his job and the constant barrage of complaints. William was only ten then, a skinny misfit, suspended between smart-aleck cracks and still playing with toys like Buzz Lightyear and a stuffed Cookie Monster that he hid when friends came over. Now, he is all grown into manhood and a successful medical practice where he spends all day examining eyes. His wife, Maura, is a petite wisp of a thing who looks like she might belong in the Ladies Auxiliary but then opens her mouth—flat country twang—and cusses like a sailor. "It's like we're on the damned *effing* Titanic," she says, with Tad standing there with his mouth open and soaking it all up. "That staircase!" she says, "and all these chaise lounges, the ferns and chandeliers." She continues, pointing out things, the rolling hallways with floral carpets, big planters and wicker, a wicker wheelchair, steamer chairs. The heavy, dark furniture is upholstered in maroon and gold and dark green and the warped floors look like a tricky Putt-Putt course, the walls so thin that the night sounds range from coughs and flushes to baby cries and the occasional wail of sex, which brings all but the frantic baby and crickets to a standstill.

By the first night, they are fully restored to their earliest roles: William, well read and up on the world but also bossy, protective, and suspicious. Suzanne, the peacekeeper, who sees herself as a free spirit but handles the role in a way that dares others to judge and reject her, like when she was insistent that the twins not get a bath of any kind for over a week. Glen said he had gone his whole life without hearing the word *vernix* (or, God forbid, *birthing custard*) and now he was hearing these daily, and yet, the paradox, because in no time these all-natural home-birthed girls were decked out in pink bows and ruffles. And finally, there is Rosie, cute and funny but with a streak of brat, and in recent years (Glen's appraisal, yet again) has never met a conspiracy theory she didn't embrace.

Drama: from the Greek *Drao*—"To do / to act." Vera once heard someone say, "It's not about what you don't do but what you do do," a line that always was successful in making the whole family laugh.

Drama. It began as a floater, the beginnings of a migraine like she had not had in years, not since she was a young woman with hormones thrown by childbirth and those exhausted moments when a safe harbor, a trusted hand to take care of her babies, allowed her to take a break, and as if on cue, as soon as she let go, the blood rushed through her head in a torrent, a haloed light eclipsing her right eye followed by a much-needed sink into darkness. It's just a migraine, she thought, a long overdue break needed. In all the years of the periodic migraines, what was consistent other than having proclaimed a day of rest, was that she always thought of the same childhood memory as she sprawled in a puddle of late afternoon light in the center of that green braided rug. She could hear her mother in the kitchen washing dishes and the sun felt so good on her body, the light in the big picture window flickering with the branches of the large dogwood tree.

By the second day, they have resurrected old sibling complaints, the jealousies, the competitions, full throttle. Each is prepared to deliver a soliloquy about life *now*, the ambitions and successes, the language particular to the expertise that leaves others slightly in the dark—OCT, strabismus, uveitis; QAnon; Python, ruby on rails—And of course there are the harder parts as well, all those bits of their lives that present hardship and would have been so much easier had things been different in childhood (had more money, more attentive parents, ate more vegetables). When

Glen can't take it anymore, he interrupts and breaks the tension with a proclamation of "Guilty! Crimes of passion! Will I get life or the chair?"

Now, William is once again expressing his fear of fire, something he has had since seeing *The Towering Inferno* when he was eight—*what were you two thinking when you rented that movie?*—and the way this great wooden structure where they are staying could go up in flames in no time. *A raging inferno*, he keeps saying, *it's a potential raging inferno*. He says that those in rooms with fireplaces are just asking for a disaster, and he knows every disaster (natural or manmade) possible and every medical emergency that can happen. He can actually explain how running with a stick *might* put your eye out and what smoke inhalation will do to your lungs. They have drawn a circle with green sharpie around the mosquito bite on Eli's leg and another where he has a bite that they have yet to identify—Tick? Flea? Some kind of spider?—to make sure that the redness or swelling doesn't spread, indicating infection. Vera refuses to look at Glen when he pinches her thigh under the table because she is practicing the model role of composure. She is a composed, loving mother at the dinner table who smiles warmly and laughs in a gentle manner. When they are alone in bed, she will tell Glen how she already wants to draw a circle around herself and stay there, either that or scream at the top of her lungs "CUT—SCENE OVER!"

"And let's talk about what happened to my Buzz Lightyear," William says, a sentence that has been said at every gathering for over twenty years.

"It started with what you did to Polly Pocket," Suzanne says.

"You put Buzz Lightyear in the toilet and he *never* talked again," William says to Suzanne.

"You tied Polly Pocket to a firecracker. You ruined her. Her arm melted and she smelled awful. You weren't batshit afraid of fire *then*."

Maura guffaws over *batshit* and then apologizes to William, who is not smiling.

"You both ruined the whole vacation," Rosie pipes up. "We were supposed to go to Story Land that day and because of you two, we didn't get to and all I got was a cheap coloring book and some M&M's from the gift shop."

"Story Land!" Now William and Suzanne reunite in laughter. "We were so sick of Story Land. How many times are you gonna ride that stupid train and pretend you're scared?"

"Well, I had never been." Rosie says this to Pete and then repeats it to Tad who nods with each word.

"You should thank us," Suzanne says. "It wasn't Disneyland, which by the way, we did *not* go to like all of our friends. I didn't get to go until I went with college friends. We are definitely taking the girls."

"GUILTY!" Glen yells. "Send me to the chair!"

They visited Suzanne and Pete not long ago—a tiny walk-up apartment in Cambridge—but chose to eat very little (*oh my, we shouldn't have had such a big breakfast*, polite lie) because they saw the kitchen. Glen found a long dark hair in the potato salad (perfect match to Pete's, who had insisted they take off their shoes at the door because he had recently visited Japan).

Organic, Glen whispered to her and stealthily left his plate on a cluttered shelf in the pantry. They were told that everything was all natural—down on fat but not concerned about random hairs and possible salmonella or so said the dirty dishrag slung on the sink; Vera had watched it administered to dirty counter, wipe and swipe, as well as the hands of Dakota who'd been picking her nose all morning, and then used as secondary oven mitt to take a casserole from the oven.

"What about booger free?" She whispered back to Glen and they both had to fake coughs to keep from choking. They could not wait to get to the bar at the Charles Hotel later that afternoon and then to order room service while they stretched out on clean cotton sheets.

The flickering. Who knew it was the first sign of this other thing, whatever it is—benign or malignant? Good or evil? Isn't the whole world split that way these days? She hasn't told anyone. Couldn't take the drama, an irony since her whole adult life has been devoted to it, forty years of teaching drama to high school students, many vacations spent in rehearsals listening to some shy kid try to make eye contact while quoting lines from *Macbeth*. It was always a challenge to see what plays she could get away with. Dare she try Albee or Stoppard? And wouldn't a little O'Neill be good for everyone in high school, so they could see dysfunction full force with the hope they might recognize it when it comes knocking on their door?

She had once even done a few choice numbers from *Hair*—nude bodysuits and wild wigs—with necessary cuts to get by the PTA. Those wonderful early-seventies kids—not much younger than Vera who was fresh out of college, though at the time, they seemed like a whole different generation; their minds were wide open, peace and love, so politically and socially moved to do something meaningful because didn't they all know, within slight degrees of separation, someone who went to Vietnam and never came home? But the shift in social awareness is so fickle, and present circumstances are what helped send her screaming and running toward retirement—even as she really wanted to stay and fight the fight as she had for years. Now, when she got a lecture from parents or principal, some prudish kid squealing on a discussion, back she'd go to *Our Town* and *The Glass Menagerie*, both well-loved favorites that teach so much of what should be known, so nothing lost, although this was a fact she always kept to herself when addressing the PTA about the importance of a broad range of knowledge and exposure.

Wouldn't you rather be in a community college, friends had often asked, *or the university branch right down the road?* But no, she liked the job of opening a door on the world for those young minds. How often had one of her students returned years later with a whole new way of seeing, and given her a little bit of credit. All those times she had said: someday you will read this or some day when *you* are a parent, when *you* are financially responsible, when *you* are aware of your own life and the parts you are playing, you will remember. *You will have so many roles*, she liked to say, *your Playbill bio will look like a phone book*, and even as she thinks that, she has to edit, because kids these days have probably never seen a phone book.

* * *

192 | Jill McCorkle

The first time they were here, there were what seemed endless hours of shuffleboard and swimming, treks up and down the huge, curious staircase, bookshelves all along the way, and the kids began leaving each other clues and messages tucked away, a whole scavenger hunt of sorts; she still has some of the slips of paper, in fact, the funny word games they liked. Rosie loved homonyms—*a tail tale, the bear was bare*—and these are the images Vera holds on to when they disagree. There was only the old original building then, the rooms rustic like in a cabin; even in late June, they wore sweaters at night. That trip was planned with the hope of giving Glen a break, a new perspective on what was making him unhappy. Was it work? Something about her?

"Can't you see it's not all about you?" he had asked. "Can you see that?" There was a stretch of several years when he said that a lot. *Can't you* see? She can't help but wonder if William was hearing it as well, soaking it up and filing away that the most important thing you can do in life is *see*.

And now, Glen is studying her as he has since they arrived. "What is it?" he asks. "A surprise? Wasn't this trip surprise enough?" He says that he can *see* there's something she isn't saying. "You're not divorcing me, are you?"

People say how no two kids have the same parents, but does that account for the vast differences there might be in children? Three kids and so different? Could sibling contrariness be enough to explain the suffering of the world? Those early experiences with rejection and rebellion? Rosie's political sway and religious convictions change as often as her underwear, but she consistently slings back the vodka or wine at dusk. Vera can't help but eye

Tad like a wild creature potentially carrying disease. She loves
him, it isn't his fault—but she really wants to throw him in a hot,
soapy tub and then feed him a big dose of Looney Tunes, take
him to the doctor for his shots—and of course he might scream
and cry but he would also be protected and leave the building
with one of those soft loopstick lollypops and the promise not
to have mumps and measles and diptheria, typhoid, small pox
and polio. She is hoping that Suzanne's twins are up to date on
everything as well, but Glen says just because they've embraced
Disney and bows the size of dinner plates doesn't guarantee this
and they should stay out of it. *This is where the right meets the
left*, he said. *That's Looney Tunes right there.*

Each child has educated them in what to do with a baby. *We
don't put them on their stomachs anymore. We don't use
bumper pads. Don't put a toy in there. They don't eat baby
food.* "We are the dark ages," she told Glen. "Everything has
changed except the baby." The baby, ironically, is exactly the
same, a warm, sweet heft of yeasty smells like something just
baked, their little milky mouths rooting like newborn kittens.

   Her class is all about change and transition—put your finger
on that emotional turn. Now the word *transition* has transi-
tioned, moving through in different ways: Brendan leaves for
the winter break and returns as Brenni, cute skirt held close
when walking to her seat. Another leaves as *she* and returns as
they, something Vera needed to have explained, an image of that
old Verizon commercial—or was it Xerox—where one singular
person morphs into the plural, like the kid in a hall of mirrors
or playing many roles at once, a cape that becomes a veil that

becomes an apron or a sling. It's all fascinating and all worth talking about if they choose to talk and if the powers that be will allow it without suspensions and firings. What more can she really teach them than that? To speak a thought and to, in turn, listen. "Just give me the chance to learn, to have it explained to me," she had said more than once. "Don't throw the baby out with the bathwater" (speaking of bathing babies), a saying that none of them understood.

But she liked explaining such things, the ways of a world where there was only enough water to fill the tub once and the man bathed first and then maybe the mama and then all the children such that the poor little baby could get lost there in the dark swirl of everyone else's dirt and get tossed out and forgotten. She liked borrowing a prompt from Thornton Wilder: "Choose the least important day of your life." And then, she asked them to write about it, what came to mind? And after they all had listed ordinary, seemingly boring things, she finished the quote: "It will be important enough." And then they read the play. Sometimes she had asked if they knew someone who had died. And of course, they all did—a grandparent, an uncle, an old neighbor or teacher, a person you don't even know by name but, all of a sudden, he is no longer there directing traffic or sweeping the hallway or waving from the corner with a sign that says HUNGRY. That assignment was to write a monologue—it could be a eulogy or it could be in the voice of the person looking back over life, as Emily does in *Our Town*. Occasionally there was a parent or a sibling dead way too soon, and she carefully pulled those kids aside after class and gave them the option of not doing the project. They could do a diorama instead, a favorite set, or perhaps they would write a scene, any scene of their choosing. Several years ago, a girl made a diorama of the cemetery in *Our Town* and put her own mother's grave there at the back, tiny artificial flowers, a headstone carved from a bar of soap. She said the best part was that her dad and brother helped.

And now Vera is seeing all of life as a play. Someone, Capote maybe, said that "Life is a moderately good play with a badly written third act." So, maybe this is Act III. Call it: *Family Gathering at the Inn*: Act I, "The Early Years"; Act II, "The Kids Leave the Nest"; Act III, "They All Return."

Set the stage. The light and sounds. The Dining Room cast in morning light, a huge round table, lazy Susan for family style, high chair, booster seats. Eggs and toast, bacon and sausage, pancakes, fruit, yogurt. Spin the wheel and there's something for everyone. She thinks of Wilder's *The Long Christmas Dinner* and the way the people come and go, aging with each turn and then exiting through the black curtain only to have the new members emerge to fill the chairs. Not the most exciting play to perform (*So depressing*, one parent said, *what on earth were you thinking?*), but the children—even those who said it was boring—had fun coming and going, the strut of youth followed by their simulated deterioration of age, stooped, bowed backs and gray wigs or canned spray they used on one another while stifling backstage laughter.

In this play, the family seeks safe topics of conversation. They tell the stories they have all heard a million times. Safe, removed from politics and philosophy. In fifth grade, William had a teacher he despised because she didn't allow free play at recess and he made up a song about her. *Miss Latha, I hate her, she'll talk and talk till your head'll fall off.* And yet, now, as Glen likes to point out when it's just the two of them, William is married to someone who can't stop talking, which is true. Vera watches the others waiting for the right time to jump in, mouths opening and then closing in surrender. *Help I've fallen and she won't shut up,* Glen said when they first met her, and they talked about how the first wife had been so quiet and they wondered if William just didn't know how to communicate, and had they somehow done this to him? He *sees* but he does not *hear.*

And then there's Pete, a little socially inept, the way he speaks too loudly and looks around to make sure he has an audience, heavy eyelids like a lizard, long hair slicked straight back; Suzanne tells them he's the most accomplished tech wizard in a three-state area. "How many times do I have to hear this lecture?" Glen whispers in her ear—"who *bit* who?"

Ah, to be able to say CUT! In class she used a kitchen timer for those who lacked self-control and liked to deliver the soliloquy to nowhere, or she would reach into the air to press what she had told them on the first day was the pause button. Pause. Pause. Pause.

Today she'd probably get fired for many of her tactics and yet, they had worked so well for so very long. Students need guidelines from people they trust. That is a fact and they need to be taught the *facts*. *Trust*—that's an important word for everyone, and what Vera knows to trust these days is that it is safest to stick to things they can all mostly agree on or have a safe difference of opinion—*I love Colin Firth* and *I love the Food Network.*

MAURA: Oh God, love Colin, but can't effin stand that shitty Food Channel and just let me tell you all the goddamn reasons why.

GLEN: What about the Navel Channel? They all love that one for sure and what's with all the *effin?* She says everything else so just say *fuck* already.

TAD: I heard that! I heard that! I heard Granddaddy say something really bad.

Of course, they can always talk about their old beloved pets; the kids all agree there, laughing, sometimes crying, telling the stories that have been told over and over. Sparky and sweet Paddy—*Knick knack paddy whack*—and old giant Elmer, part St. Bernard, who always smelled fishy, moving like a big bear crawling from some primordial stew, loping slue-footed onto Rosie's bed. Or Monique the otherwise absolutely perfect poodle with the anal gland problem, her dignified name reduced to Scoot. And what about the fish cemetery and the guinea pigs who accidentally inbred and then their babies bumbled around with problems that were all her fault. She felt so responsible for that terrible biological accident. Who knew that the procreation could happen that fast—the male placed with the female just long enough for Vera to shake new pine shavings and scoop away the soiled ones. Then there was the cat who loved to bring Glen bird parts as if she knew he was the one with the hobby, cleaning and tending the many feeders. Glen put a bell so big—a sleigh bell meant for the Christmas tree, Suzanne added—that poor Stella walked with her head lowered to the ground. "Catch something down there," Glen had told her, "a bug or snake."

When the conversation heads in the wrong direction, Vera tells about their favorite neighbor Arlene's cat, Rascal, who she and Glen both love, a huge handsome Norwegian Forest cat who runs like a dog to greet them when they visit, and then swings from the curtains in Arlene's living room; he thinks his name is *Stop It* because that's what everyone—especially Tad, who Rascal likes to stalk—says to him. "I can't believe Dad likes spending time with that cat after what he did to poor Stella," Suzanne says, and Glen says it's because Rascal outweighs him. He also says that he and Rascal—unlike many people in his life—agree on most things, and because like grandchildren, Rascal isn't with them full-time.

Things, simple things, or people of the past—Miss Latha, or Mr. Thomas, a long-ago neighbor rumored to have taken whatever pills were left in his old prescriptions on New Year's Eve. There was almost always an ambulance involved. Or what about that person who showed up saying he was Glen's childhood friend and then after spending two nights realized his friend's last name wasn't Wiley but Walters. What was his name? Loved bourbon and stole William's Backstreet Boys CD.

"I never had a Backstreet Boys CD," he says to Maura.

"That's right," Suzanne says. "It was Hanson."

Vera's early memory is there daily now, a fleeting dream she tries to grasp and hold: the light, the voices—not singular but plural, a chorus of voices calling out to her alone. It's there and then it's gone, just light through the window; her mother is in the kitchen, water running in the sink, soapy suds and steam on the window, red gingham dishcloth and her mother's warm, damp hands patting her head when she reaches up to hold on to the belt of her blue dress, the voices and light behind her in the other room.

When William was born, he had a stork bite, that's what they called it, little red birthmark at the base of his neck, and she noticed it first thing; when they brought him back to her from the nursery, she looked for it, placing her finger on it, that bit of proof like a label that he belonged to her. He and Suzanne had fought for years it seemed, their bickering back and forth, doors slamming—*Give me a break! Which bone? Name the bone!*— part of the rhythm of the house, even though they had a lot in common, only a year apart and through high school sharing many friends and activities. Even now it continues, their spouses sighing their *oh no, not again* sighs.

"Remember when Mom caught you watching porn on the family computer?" Suzanne has *reminded* him of this before, like every time they are in the same room for more than an hour.

"One time. That happened one time and you know what really happened."

"We know what you *said*."

"I was looking up the White House for a school report." He looks at Suzanne's twins, three years old with those bows as big as their heads, off to one side as if they are following the conversation instead of what they're really doing, which is seeing how much catsup can be squirted onto a plate. "Homework," he tells Eli, who looks just like his mother, including that sarcastic smirk, "and I didn't know to put *dot gov* instead of *dot com*. And what's more," he turned back to his sister, "even if I had wanted to enjoy it, how could I with all the bad dialogue? Can't you just imagine Mom correcting the grammar or saying 'how stupid.' Who are these people? Somebody needs to tell them to say: 'This is what I'm GOING to do to you, not gonna.'"

Then they are off to a discussion of Glen's Uncle Ron, who had a stash of smut in his garage that the children found hidden under old *Life* and *Look* magazines, things so bad that Suzanne later had to talk to a therapist to get over having seen the pictures, and all the while the man's wife was in the kitchen, drinking coffee, her cup easily marked with the coral smudge of her lipstick, and smoking those long brown More cigarettes and reeling off a litany of who was sick and dying and of what. She began a lot of sentences with "Now don't laugh because this isn't funny," and then how could it not be? The children sitting there, shoulders shaking and red in the face, as they tried not to laugh. "What's funny? I said a broken hip," she said with a stream of smoke. "That's the kiss of death. Right? Everybody knows that's the kiss of death, that's what they say, the kiss of death." Vera had a hard time not laughing herself and that's why she sent the children out of the room in the first place so they wouldn't set her off; Glen was safely watching football in the next room with Ron, and Rosie was just a baby crawling after one of several cats sprawled on the backs of chairs.

"What about when you threw away my flowers from the homecoming dance?" Suzanne asks, coming back in for another round.

"They were dead," William says, "and they stank. And you hung them over the desk we had to share and the pollen was getting on my work and you didn't even like Tony Martone." He explains to Pete that Tony Martone was a jerk who got caught cheating on the proficiency test in junior high. "That's your competition."

"He owns his own business and has made millions," Suzanne said.

"And no one is sure what he *really* does."

If Vera were going to break the fourth wall, she would stand and face the many people gathered there in the Inn dining room, knife blade tapping her crystal water glass, and say: *Here you see what appears to be a normal extended family gathered for a celebration*—and she would gesture to the large round table in the corner—husband, son, two daughters and their families, lazy Susan piled with dishes suddenly still, stopped for this announcement to the silent listeners. *But what they don't know, Dear Viewer*—she would narrate, in kind of a Rod Sterling voiceover—*and what they will soon learn, is that this is a goodbye party of sorts, their mother beginning the final leg of life's journey. The curtain is rising and Act III has begun . . .*

Eli now has four green circles on his body and Tad, who looks up to him, has started drawing around his own bug bites as well as any freckle or mole; he looks just like that Dr. Seuss animal in a book Rosie once loved, *Put Me in the Zoo*. Vera mentions this but none of them find it as funny as she had hoped. She mentions how Rosie loved homonyms and they made up little verses, but Rosie sighs in a dismissive way. The year before, they had kept

Tad while Rosie and Derek were on "an important retreat" but they were afraid to ask what the "retreat" was for. By then, there were a lot of things they didn't talk about, and no *hart heart* or *dear deer* was going to change it.

"What's another word for 'stupid'?" Tad had asked while there and Glen told him to just listen to his grandmother when the president was talking and he would get a lot of words. He later came back to give a report, all written in crayon and misspelled: *moran, stoog, idiat, lunytic, ashole.* He stopped and held the paper to his chest, waiting to see if *ashole* would bring a reprimand, but no, Glen just nodded and said that was good work.

Now, Tad will be going into second grade and remembers all the words he learned in their care, something that Rosie has brought up a couple of times, and which is why now Tad reports everything he hears. When Tad mentions at the dinner table what he now calls the Grandma stupid list, Glen says, "But be sure you clarify, that was the *other* president."

"The one mom voted for," he says and Rosie, sitting across from them, gives a thumbs up, and in one swift moment Glen looks at Vera as if to say, what now? He pinches her thigh *too* hard, taking out on her his restraint. They have made a pact to get through the weekend. Rosie is their daughter. They love her. They love Tad—tattler that he is—even though Tad is at that awkward age, reverting, when younger kids are around, to pretend baby talk and a kind of neediness that requires an enormous amount of patience. As stage director, Vera would inform the audience: *It's a painful, yet consistent stage of human development.*

* * *

She had come to see so much of life as theater. Shift the light / slow the speech—linger here. Does this happen offstage, leaving lust or grief or death to the imagination of the audience, or is it public? Vera thinks of all the soliloquies of life—all she never really wanted to share and yet the words are there, spoken on that stage within her mind, the spotlight that pulls her into focus like that long-ago memory. And what does a person do with such a memory, something that has never been told? Do you give it voice or do you take it with you, tuck it away safely as it has always been, that lucky thing you carry in your pocket. *You will be fine, dear.* Had they called her dear? These voices in chorus, or had she added that along the way? *You will be fine.* In her own memory play, this is her moment, the one she has thought of her whole life when the light is just so, and for a fleeting moment there is a euphoric sense of immortality. *You will have a good life.*

The success of her teaching drama is that she didn't allow *drama.* No hysteria, no histrionics, you act. The more subtle, the better. The tilt of the head, the set of the mouth. The better, more serious students got this and when they did, they saw how overacting was a mockery of something important, examples being the girl who goes screeching each time she sees a spider or roach, the one who slips into hyperbole and extreme descriptions. *The worst, the best, you always, you never,* all those things that are heard on the news, all those things they tell you to avoid in therapy if what you want is to have an honest working relationship. The best actors know this. They know the power of the unknown, the respect that must be given to it. And isn't this what it's about? The moment of stillness. This moment of awareness? Spotlight this. And then this.

"I'll use my ninja star to get you!" Tad says, and Glen makes a scary face and says, "Do it." Glen says: "Do it and draw back a nub." He laughs a scary laugh their own children had loved and looks at Eli who isn't sure which side he's on. "That'll be a big circle," he says, but Tad is already running off to his mother. "He said he'd give me a nub!" Tad screams. Glen knows better than to tease like that; they've talked about it, but it's like he just can't help himself after several hours of not saying anything while Tad tattles and Eli asks worried questions about the world and the twins squirt condiments and giggle like munchkin stereo.

Perhaps this is where she should call for intermission—*Please go get a drink folks, walk around, enjoy the lovely lobby.* There is a woman standing there who looks so familiar to Vera even though she is sure they've never met, the woman so removed from this generation, wearing what should be called a frock like Vera's old grandmother who died in Vera's childhood, the heft of her body, breasts to the waist, a farm wife of the thirties, stubby fingers like little Vienna sausages, her hair in oiled ringlets. The woman's presence is puzzling, a time warp, a flicker that again takes her back to that warm circle of light, to the braided rug, the dogwood tree, the flicker of light.

She can stand right over there, the elevator leading into the dining room, crystal goblet once again in hand, the chime of her knife—*May I have your attention?* She herself will find a quiet spot, perhaps an overstuffed chair, worn velvet cushions filled with the down of a goose centuries old—the dust motes she has told her students to avoid waxing about, there in the slant of light doing what they do to everyone, filling her with a wave of nostalgia that is now cliché from overuse, yes, but also universal—something caught in art for thousands of years, a wave of a wand, a sprinkling of magic dust, that ethereal, slanting passage to heaven. *Taking an intermission* she will grab Glen's warm hand as he passes, the callous of his thumb a reminder of all that has led them here—blunt, strong fingers designed for work. They have both worked hard through the years.

"You must be honest," she always told her students, "You're seeking truth," and she usually quoted from Tennessee Williams's opening monologue in *The Glass Menagerie*: "'I give you truth in the pleasant disguise of illusion.'"

"Truth!" she told them, arms opened wide. "It may be all wrapped up in drama and exaggerations but in the center, that rich dark center, is *truth*. Chew on it, let it stick."

"You make it sound like we're eatin' Milk Duds," one boy had said and guffawed, then smacked in an annoying way the rest of the term. "Just chewin' like you said to do, Miz Dubya."

"Stop trying to figure them all out and make them get along," Glen has said too many times to count when she has expressed hope for a future day when William was not so driven and hard and when Suzanne was not so judgmental about Vera's leather shoes and occasional hamburger, and Rosie no longer dressed like she was about to do a pole dance, but settled and comfortable with her intelligent mind (sigh). And once she gets on a roll, it's hard to stop: maybe William will have gone to therapy and forgiven his father for *not* having a silver spoon to shove in his mouth and forgiven *her* for all the times she assumed he was responsible and capable and therefore didn't need all the extra attention that his sisters, who were louder and more expressive, were demanding, and Rosie, sweet little Rosie. *Hart and hind— heartlessly hindered—dear deer.*

Don't suck the life out of me, she has thought on more than one occasion, but who do you say that to? All she wants is a tiny bit of life, like the Host on the tongue, or the long-ago sugar cube that kept her safe from polio. She had grown up with someone who bore the scars, misshapen leg and jaw. She had lived to see eradication and yet where would people like her daughter lead them? Now when the topic comes up, Glen can't help himself and says that he's decided not to get the rabies shot for Lucy because it frightens her; she trembles at the vet anyway and a shot would terrify her, and besides, he doesn't know exactly what is in the shot anyway. "Lucy has her rights," he says and though William and Maura are biting back smiles and Suzanne and Pete are staring out the window, Rosie is flushed and looks like she wants to run from the table; but no one crosses the big, hefty line Glen has put down, not even Derek, who is beating his spoon on the table in an angry rhythmic beat like the prelude to something about to explode. It's clear he's tempted but he is also enjoying the biking and hiking this free vacation offers.

Glen's comments have hit them all; he has talked about entitlement and how disgusting it is and he has talked about being so superior that you are all judgment with no compassion or forgiveness for people who didn't have the same advantages. He has spoken his own soliloquy, asking them how they think the world can possibly survive at this rate, and when Eli, alarm in his eyes, asks does he think the aliens are coming or a disease or nukes or what, Glen says, the aliens came long ago, which sets both boys off, Tad saying he will use his ninja star and kill them and Eli asking for the facts where and when, *Please, what are you talking about*; the twins, thankfully, are once again lost under their big bows and playing the catsup game. The grown-ups remain silent even though Vera knows they will all get to their rooms as quickly as possible and fume and vent and chatter on into the night about how their parents never change, same old same old, why did they even think this trip might be different, and no doubt Tad will deliver some details later as he always does (*Derek said four words I'm not supposed to say*) and though Vera sometimes feels guilty for egging on her little *double naught* agent, she will offer cake or cookie and listen. *Oh really? Oh my. How about that.*

You will be loved. You will be fine, dear.

These children. They *study*. They *meditate*. They *pray*. Vera and Glen have watched them rotate in and out of this or that religion. One frying latkes, another getting baptized—sprinkle, immersion—rosaries swinging from the rearview, bobblehead Buddha on the dash—*namaste*. There have been family dinners dominated by philosophical debates; Vera and Glen have been accused of doing too much (*It's my life. You had your turn*) and then accused of not doing enough (*I really could have used a tutor. Everybody else had a car. You were out of town when I had appendicitis*) until she could tell Glen had taken all that he could take. *Just shut up and be nice*, he said. *Just do the right goddamn thing!*

Vera never wanted to be their best friend; she only wanted to be their mother. She chose to be their mother and she wanted to do and say all the things mothers do and say. *Don't pick your nose! Chew with your mouth closed. Don't cheat, lie, or steal. Wash your hands and brush your teeth. Don't do drugs. Be aware of those less fortunate. I really hope people won't fuck you over or break your heart, but it is almost certain that someone will find a way to do it, so please, please, please, after it's all over, don't protect yourself so much you stop taking chances. You will come out the other side better, wiser, stronger. It's an inoculation of sorts. You will be vaccinated against assholes because they will always be there, and you deserve better.* Ahh, that is her soliloquy, delivered so often to tired old Lucy, who has her own story, gray around the face, and though protected from rabies, still mourning her sister, Ethel.

She told her class when they read *Death of a Salesman*: "We hear a crash, a terrible sound, and we imagine the scene in the distance, Willy's car wrapped around a tree. We don't think of a teenager in black slamming trash can lids—we don't imagine a wall heaped with boxes and props and the textbooks for all their homework assignments. We see Willy Loman. We see a road and a hopeless man on it."

"But that's not in the story," a boy in her class had said. "It says nothing like all you just made up and said." He had a snuff patch in his gum, thinking she didn't notice, and a few hairs on his chin he wanted people to notice, also called a patch. A soul patch.

"What?"

"The part you just made up."

"It's called projection. What could be. Your imagination is founded on and fueled by this principle."

"Could be don't count," he said. "My daddy said 'could be' don't pay no bills." That was twenty years ago and who knows where that boy landed, who knows what he might now have tucked and hidden from view—Handgun? Hypodermic? Deceit? Or maybe he came through, met an enlightened friend who pulled him into a new place. Maybe he was lucky enough to figure out Daddy *could* be wrong. Daddy *don't know* everything.

The first time they ever came here, Vera still used a diaphragm and she and Glen laughed at all those old jokes about things you could do with an old one. Shower cap for your cat. Doorknob cover. And then there was no uterus at all, an empty cavity where once, according to Rosie, there was a dark, warm room with a radio. And sweet little Rosie with her endless homonyms: *Feet and feat. Heart and hart. Dear and deer. Thyme and time.*

Tad points at Glen, mouth set in an angry straight line: "He called my daddy a maladroit misanthrope!"

"I never said that." Glen looks at her and shrugs, the mischief in his eyes as alive as when they were thirty. "I don't even know what that means, son. You must've heard that on TV."

"You did, too, and Eli's mom says that pond might give you Effin E Cola." Glen says he prefers to have "A Cola." He says, "How about a Pepsi cola?"

Since going to the doctor, and learning that something in her head is different, Vera has had glimpses of the past appearing as vividly as photographed moments. There they are: she and Glen are so young. Would there ever be anything better than that tiny deck on their first rental house? About a decade ago, they had agreed that some of their very best times were those Friday afternoons early in their marriage when they bought a six-pack of beer and sat out on a deck barely big enough for two chairs while conjuring the future. The pulse. The pause. The anticipation of all that lay ahead. She's so glad they realized and glad they have made the effort to reenact those times. It's why now he has suggested they go out in one of the boats while the others are napping or plugged into their various devices.

"So, I can tell there's something you want to say," he says, once they push off from the dock and are moving.

"Just that I'm glad we did this, glad everyone is here."

"Even with the pains in the ass?"

"Perhaps because of them." She had thought this would be a good time to fill him in, but no, why ruin such a perfect scene? And it is perfect, the water, the light; it's almost too perfect to be real, which is why they need Tad there on the shore waving his notepad—circles all over those skinny white legs—and screaming for them to come back and get him. They smile at each other and keep rowing.

"We've done okay haven't we?"

"Yes, we've done okay."

"Then why so serious?"

Someday, everything will change, so let them argue. Let them spew their words of anger. If not in the near future, then someday death will hit the pause button and they will freeze like in that game they once played in the side yard. *Freeze—you're it,* she heard them call and wouldn't she love to be there now, the old webbed yard chair leaving indentations on her young pudgy thighs, the sprinkler fanning back and forth, their garden barely started, Glen's old Impala leaking oil on the concrete drive they had saved to pave, a blank canvas for future chalk drawings and skateboard ramps and a basketball hoop. *Freeze.*

And what will their world be like without her? Will they wonder how she and Glen managed to do all that they have done? Will they see her life as she desires it to be seen there in the quiet moment of retrospective kindness the intermission will bring? She stares at the old hotel, afternoon sunlight glinting on the many windows, some open, some closed, and she pulls back with the thought, oar resting on her thighs.

"Letting me do all the work?"

"Yes, dear."

But now is not the time to mention anything, not today, not during this bright spot. Life is always moving toward death; literature speaks this truth again and again, and yet, it is still a shock to look out and see the landing strip within view, the tiny lights leading and pulling her forward. She likes to think that leaving will be like breaking the fourth wall, stepping down-stage into the footlights and then out of view.

Of that first trip, the kids recall black flies and a muddy lake, new Juicy jeans caught in a bicycle chain, a sprained ankle (*You don't remember?*), it rained the first half of the week (*You don't remember?*). Asthma and chiggers. It was freezing at night. Suzanne had a nosebleed in the dining room—*You blew up my Polly Pocket. You put my Buzz Lightyear in the toilet. We didn't get to go to Story Land because of you two. I hated you for that. Mom called Dad something bad in French and Dad smoked so much Mom went to the laundromat to wash clothes, saying we all smelled like the inside of an ashtray. Then Mom cried and skipped breakfast; she said she had a migraine. Rosie vomited in the car. No I didn't, that was a different trip. Yes. No. Yes.*

But now, here on the glistening water, a calm comes over her as Glen's arms propel them forward across the lake—*You will be fine, dear*—the sun is warm on her face, and she closes her eyes to that long-ago flickering scene, water running, voices calling, as she crawls and reaches toward that puddle of light.

✳ Sparrow

The news would have been shocking anywhere but seemed especially so in a town like ours, or so we liked to believe: a young mother choosing to asphyxiate herself and infant son in the family Volvo while her husband was at work in the city and their daughter in preschool at the Episcopal Church. Everyone knew who she was, had seen her at Whole Foods or Dunkin' Donuts or the car pool line, the young, fresh-faced woman in sweatpants and comfortable shoes, hair yanked up in a high ponytail, a look common enough among the pregnant and newly postpartum. Like me, the young family had lived there for over a year but still were thought of as new people: the people from Delaware; the people who bought the pretty red

Cape with a century-old rose garden and basement that flooded every spring when the snow melted and the nearby river crested its bank. "Do they know about the basement?" people wondered with follow-ups of personal testimonies about French drains and sump pumps. "Do they know about tending roses?"

Those are the years when, if not a native of a place, you know the parents of children in your own children's classes, the mailman, the regulars at your local market. The world revolves around your elementary school and then gets bigger when your children enter junior high and then high school, bigger and more complicated. But at this time it was simple: two kids, one school, one bus picking up and dropping off with impressive regularity. Ballet on Wednesdays and karate on Monday and violin on Thursday. Come spring, Little League would practice often with games in the late afternoon. The calendar was all filled in for us—busy but simple, and someone going through upheaval needs simple. One year divorced and barely settled into this new life, simple days were a vacation.

But the stories circulating about the young family from Delaware who lived in the beautiful red Cape, now forever tainted by the tragedy, were not simple at all. There was no note; there was a whole chicken simmering in a crockpot on the kitchen counter; there were clothes still in the washing machine; the television was on and tuned to the Disney Channel. It was as if the idea was sudden, impulsive. Maybe she got a phone call, someone mused, or found something in the house that flipped her switch. Maybe she staged it to make it look like they were victims of a crime. She had left a beautifully wrapped birthday present for her daughter, who would turn three the next week, and there was a home hair-coloring kit on the bathroom sink. Someone heard the husband was having an affair. Someone heard the young mother had a history of depression (*and who doesn't?* one woman asked). The word *postpartum* was whispered, especially if there was a pregnant woman nearby and it seemed in those years that there was *always* a pregnant woman nearby. There were other details I tried not to hear, fearing that the end of her life would undermine what was the beginning of my new one.

I'd loved this town at first sight: the river, the easy access to the city, the winding roads—stone walls that had been there for over a century. It felt safe. I loved the quiet reserve of the people here—friendly but not too friendly—you could have distance if you wanted and I did want that. I needed that. It was a great place to raise kids. Everyone said that and it was true. Just passing the sign each day that welcomed me to the town brought a great sigh of relief. There was a Victorian house there at the busy intersection coming into town where a bedsheet hung on the porch, often flapped in the wind, its painted messages heralding an upcoming event: *Lordy lordy, look who's forty*, *'Tis the season*, or *For he's a jolly good fellow*. With the news of the tragedy, a plain black sheet had hung for weeks, a gesture of grief for the whole community.

I had spent a childhood saying *if only it would snow*. From November to February, I studied the southern winter sky for some fleck that might lead to a slight dusting and that mad race to the grocery store to stock up on bread and milk and batteries as if the nuclear winter had arrived. If only it would snow, and now many miles and years from that place, New England granted my wish often and regularly, and still I felt great excitement and awe each time. It buffered and insulated us, shrouded the small white frame house where I lived with my son and daughter. There was a glassed-in porch across the front that I had lit with mini lights, and there was old wicker porch furniture, a glider that had once been my grandmother's draped in loose chintz fabrics. Paint and fabric had become a great distraction for me during the divorce, the Benjamin Moore sample wheel my Bible.

I often studied the paint chips there on the porch in the bright winter daylight, looking up occasionally to wave to those passing by on our busy street; the living room would be October Mist or Zenful; the dining room, Mediterranean Spice. Pistachio for the kitchen, and I would use accents of red and pink, a combination that reminded me of the caladium bulbs and spider lilies that had once filled my grandmother's side yard. I was drawn to the small kitchens I remembered from my childhood, shiny Formica and speckled floors, cozy breakfast nooks as opposed to the newly-embraced stainless and granite and mile-long islands that put me more in mind of a laboratory or morgue. I wanted a retro refrigerator in pink; I wanted odd pieces of dime-store china. The house had wonderful old radiators that clanged and hissed at different tempos, like animals chained to the wall.

At Christmas we pretended we were in a movie, decorating the tree there on the porch, Marly whirling up and down in her nightgown as Clara from *The Nutcracker* while Evan studied his Game Boy. I had reached back to reclaim what I recalled from childhood, big colored bulbs and shiny strands of silver tinsel we all threw by the handfuls. *This is our movie*, I often thought. *This is a happy part.* My daughter's roles were many: Cinderella and Sleeping Beauty, Little Red Riding Hood. *Oh my what big eyes you have.* She pretended to be the miller's daughter in *Rumpelstiltskin* having to spin straw into gold, sticks and leaves put through her makeshift spindle (an old tire from their Big Wheel) and pulling out strands of tinsel or fake coins. She wanted me to make mean, ugly-voiced demands that she spin that straw into gold. Then I also had to dance around and sing in a scary voice: *Nobody knows but my name is Rumpelstiltskin. Rumpelstiltskin.*

We had to choose a word at the elementary school. A secret word that a parent would always give if sending someone to get his or her child in an emergency. Children were taught to ask: *What is the secret word?* They were taught never to go otherwise. It was several years before the irony occurred to me, that our secret word to ensure safety came from a story about someone trying to take a child away from its parents.

The days grew longer and warmer, the school bus wheezing up and stopping right on schedule; it seemed that the fewer clothes the children needed as they emerged from their cocoons of coats and hats and boots, the busier their schedules became. Little League was my greatest relief that spring—a legitimate pause in the day—and armed with yard chair, I tried to make myself a part of the scene but not. The games usually took place behind the elementary school, a sprawling red brick structure surrounded by suburbia. It was not unusual for the man whose yard adjoined the field to appear from behind a hedge of Ligustrum and toss balls back onto the field. Evan was in fourth grade, and Marly, kindergarten—perfect distance so that there would not be double college tuition in a year. We had actually thought about things like that. We'd thought about all the practical details of a day: clean clothes laid out and lunches packed in Spiderman and Little Mermaid containers, money set aside for braces, summer camps, and other activities. What we did not plan or anticipate was the way distance can grow and separate what once was strong and how life can take two nice and loving people and urge them to move in different directions, the early blame and judgments really just ways to avoid the hurtful truth that what once was is no more. And then the worst part of all, the scene you will never ever want replayed, that afternoon that clearly defines the before and after. You say the words to your children and watch their faces—this one was just asking for chocolate milk and that one wants you to take the itchy tag from her shirt—but then there are tears and a ball kicked across the room and by the end of the day, many dents from a baseball in the garage door and perplexing questions like will we still eat dinner tonight? Will Santa still come and know where to go? Will people call us something different? Will our teachers change?

The death of the young mother and her son was still the most whispered topic but had left everyone needing to catalog other tragedies and crimes that had come before. A girl who died of an overdose, a young man who hung himself in his mother's laundry room, swastikas spray-painted on a bridge near the temple, a body found in the woods two towns over.

There was the story of the young boy who had disappeared from a local playground thirty years ago. It was the town legend as well as being the cautionary tale all parents reminded their kids about as they headed out for the day. A young portrait of innocence lifted away by evil. There was a shrine in the elementary school: an empty desk, his name carved into the wooden top. This was his last seat, people would say, children too young to fathom kidnapping left to marvel the desecration of school property. They knew that in life he would have been punished and yet, in death, grown-ups grew teary-eyed as they walked past. It had been thirty years, his family long moved away, and still his name was whispered, as if to protect him from whatever horror life had presented.

A woman named Erica had grown up there and recalled the boy in life; she remembered seeing him walk the very path to and from school where he was last seen. She had been in junior high school when it happened, just as I would have been all those miles away, my junior high housed in the crumbling building where my parents had once attended high school, where my thoughts were on summer and fitting in. I had never heard of this town or the many other places and schools that a young, conscientious guidance counselor would later introduce me to with a display of maps and brochures. Erica's son was the Little League's pitcher and doing very well at it. He was known for his encyclopedic knowledge of the Red Sox and had all the boys on the team falling into superstitions about how everything had to be done, like the way he needed to adjust his hat before each pitch and then, with great authority, spit off to the side in a way the others tried to copy.

Erica said that someone who'd worked with the husband said the young family had moved to town in hopes of a fresh start. By then many people had decided that the act was one of anger, a way to leave a marriage with a big *fuck you*. "Not that we all don't have our problems," someone said, and it seemed they looked at me with this, the one divorced person in a sea of domestic peacefulness. As kids got older, there were many homes broken and reassigned—but that spring, I was the lone example among that particular set of grade school parents; I was what you might become if you chose a path other than death. It was like I carried a disease—contagious with domestic unrest— and people needed to keep a safe distance.

I once thought I saw the boy who had disappeared, or what I had imagined was him after all the stories, his thin slouch and rusty hair. I was about to call out when he turned and caught my eye and I realized how ridiculous—this was a boy and that was thirty years ago. He had become the local martyr and people always thought they'd seen him or the man he would have become if his life had not been interrupted. And there were threats of interruption everywhere: icy sidewalks and empty wooded shortcuts, lone disheveled men, lean howling coyotes just beyond domestic tranquility, house cats and small dogs lost to the wild on a regular basis. *Thank God it wasn't a child*, people often said. *It could have been a child*. I often heard the coyotes with their high-pitched yips as I looked out on the dark woods behind our small house through the kitchen window. The kitchen was so small there was no dishwasher, so I'd gone back to the old-fashioned sudsy sink and a foam brush. There was something peaceful in the quiet ritual, my reflection against the darkness, the dual vision of safe comfort and unknown fear. Behind us was a wild expanse of woods, and in front of us, a busy street leading to the turnpike. What waited in the woods or along the highway? What lay buried at the bottom of frozen ponds and rivers that might or might not be unearthed in the future? The known and the unknown of our history, something I had prompted my junior high students to think about for over a decade. Even the least motivated of students was drawn to unsolved crimes and mysteries, bodies never found or those discovered thousands of years after the fact, like the Yde girl or Tollund Man.

One of the women, always seated on the bench right behind the backstop, was the grandmother of the boy who played third base, her clapping always loudest when he did something—his name, Patrick, constantly on her tongue. I assumed that she was visiting from out of town because I hadn't noticed her before and there was no way you would *not* notice this woman: a shock of gray, wiry hair that she clipped on either side with the same kind of little plastic barrettes my daughter wore, and a loose green cardigan with worn suede sleeves. Her eyebrows were perpetually raised, pale blue eyes wide, as if she were about to ask a question or express surprise; the furrows in her forehead were deep from years of this animated expression, exaggerated each time she leaned close to hear better. Her laugh—high and girlish—invited others to join in. Patrick's mother was very ill, and I could imagine how this feisty little woman had swooped into their darkened home with a burst of light. I took an immediate liking to her, her outspoken opinions often very funny and providing the comic relief everyone needed.

By then, we had heard that the other father had already packed up his house and daughter and returned to his native Delaware. A FOR SALE sign was out in the front yard and spring had—as so many had predicted—flooded the empty basement.

Patrick's grandmother knew other boys as well and called out to them: "Go Harry!—oh yeah, go Jason!" And for our benefit she did a running commentary on the opposition: "Is there a hole in your glove?" She always tucked her pants in her socks to keep out the mosquitoes. "You ever get that creepy feeling something is getting on you?" She fixed her gaze on me. "You know what I mean?"

Her phrases often ended that way—*you know what I mean?* or *am I right?*

I noticed others tried not to sit near her, including Patrick's dad, who often stood at the back of the group talking to a couple of other dads. I figured she and I had something in common by our aloneness. Like her, I was from the South and used to people talking to whoever would listen. I'd spent my whole life that way, people who couldn't get from point A to point B without a couple of history lessons and several anecdotes. The first game day, after I responded to something she said, she scooted her chair a little closer. I had a bag of pretzels and, seeing this, she inched even closer, then claimed this same spot each following game.

"You have nothing to worry about with your boy," she told me that day. "He is fine, a great kid. He's a natural. As long as he doesn't cheat like Pete Rose, he'll be fine." I just smiled and thanked her and she reached her hand into the pretzels. "Go Evan!" she screamed and then looked at me and smiled. What had I said that showed my worry? Patrick's grandmother was a little high-maintenance but also just what I needed. My own mother had always voiced her opinions in a similar way and so I fell right into a very old routine of listening just enough not to hurt her feelings while keeping a few cards close to my chest. After years of complaining about my mother, I missed her calls and interruptions, the advice I chose not to take.

It was around this same time we heard a different version of what happened to the young mother and the baby. She'd pulled into the garage and then left him sleeping in his car seat while she took things inside; they had had many long, sleepless, difficult nights, and so she decided to let him sleep a tiny bit longer, keep the heat running because it was so cold outside, a day barely in the twenties.

She left the car running? Someone asked. Didn't she know better?

But what about the mistress? Was that part true?

"Assume makes an ass of 'u' and 'me,'" Patrick's grandmother said. And then there was silence, everyone needing time to erase the portrait that had been painted so vividly and retrace; perhaps there was a phone call, a washing machine, a television report, a chicken to cook—perhaps she'd sat for just a second to look at her to-do list and there in a slant of warm sunlight, still bundled in her winter coat, she'd allowed her eyes to close just for a drowsy second, to give into the weight of warmth and fatigue. And who could not imagine the shock and horror of waking when you never meant to doze off and who could not forgive the instinct to then crawl into that backseat and remain. She could never have forgiven herself. Anytime anyone said: *how could you forget?* To blow out the candle, to lock the door, to turn off the stove, feed the cat, raise the thermostat, buy the dishwashing liquid, give your child his lunch money. How could you forget?

I can't bear this, one mother whispered, her infant swaddled to her chest. We all were quiet for the rest of the game, polite quietness, *Do you have the time? Do you know how many outs?* Two parents sat looking over lists, perhaps all the things they could not afford to forget. Patrick's grandmother finally offered relief when she fixed her attention on the woman who always showed up in riding pants, then stood off to the side, tapping a foot and jingling keys, Chanel bag looped over one arm, cell phone up to her ear. Patrick's grandmother motioned her over and she approached and then stopped several feet away, eyebrow raised in an irritated way.

"You look like you ride horses."

"Yes."

"Men and horses are a whole lot alike. Am I right?" she leaned forward in her chair. "You know, easy to give the wrong signal. You know what I mean. I can tell now, don't be shy."

The woman smirked and nodded and began to turn away, but Patrick's grandmother continued. She had an audience, all of us listening but trying to pretend we were completely fixated on the game. "It's all in the hands and the thighs, right? Give the wrong signal with those hands or thighs and he's off and running, am I right?" She threw back her head and laughed, reached up and reclipped her little barrette. "Of course, a horse is more likely to hear 'whoa' and stop. And of course, a horse will remember." She said this a little louder, knowing it would get a laugh, and then she pointed her finger at the woman, who by then had already turned and was walking back to stand by her car. Patrick's dad and the other men just shook their heads and then Patrick hit a homerun and everyone was cheering. "That boy needs all the good things he can get right now," she whispered to me, her raspy breath tinged with spearmint, against my ear. She always had a pocket full of that old hard Christmas candy I had never liked. "He can run like an antelope, can't he? Go Patrick!"

A lot had happened in my own life over the past few years—not just the divorce, but also the death of my father and decline of my mother, a new job in a new school, kids adjusting to the move, all the things that are on that test a therapist might give that would indicate you are worthy of a breakdown. But who had time to even *take* the test much less *have* a breakdown? It seemed best to plod forward like a mule in blinders, each dig of the plow, progress. All the days of those years bled and ran together—mountains of snow and movies like *Aladdin* in dark theaters, money slipped under pillows to retrieve the tiny teeth that left them lisping and spraying soft syllables until the sturdy grown-up one came in in ways that promised a future need of braces. We'd started our own traditions for this new segment of life. Santa Claus would leave Evan's toys in the green chair by the tree and Marly's on the sofa. Along with the big colored lights and strands of tinsel, we decorated with the kids' artwork from school and little Polaroids of them sitting on Santa's lap in the mall. We embraced any reason for a celebration. We greeted each other with "Rabbit Rabbit" on the first day of every month, took bets on Groundhog Day and the prediction to follow, strung valentines and red and pink heart lights out on the porch. We already had sparklers for Fourth of July and Halloween lights and decorations for October. It was hard to compete with the house where the big sheets hung, but I was doing my best. Come spring and summer, I would still find slivers of silver tinsel in the cracks and crevices of the old house, clinging to the feet of the radiators, shining from the depths of the compost heap, proof that it had all happened.

"Live in a place long enough and you can make a living going to funerals. Ballgames and funerals," Patrick's grandmother said, and then as she overheard a bit of conversation that included the word *depression* she was off and running in that direction. "Some catch depression from others. He knows what I mean." She motioned over to Patrick's dad. We knew that his wife was not doing well, and I assumed Patrick's games were their one outing, a block of time that might even seem normal. I wondered if the grandmother was mother or mother-in-law to the dying woman but chose not to ask for fear I'd get more information than I wanted.

I smiled at Patrick's dad as if to say *I've got you covered.*

"But depressed is better than psycho, right? Like then he'd just kill himself instead of all those children, like that awful Mama that drove her babies into a lake to be with a man."

Shhhhhhh.

"A man though!" She sighed. "She cared more for a man. She shouldn't have had babies to drown in the first place. There was another one that did that, too. Right? No mother should ever choose a man over her baby."

Shhhhhhh.

But when Evan jammed his finger, she was the one offering the most attention and advice. "Your boy needs to ice that—he also needs some confidence. It'll come—don't you worry a bit. It'll come. He's like my boy that way." That night we sat on the glider on the porch, his finger under a bag of frozen peas, and watched the cars passing. I knew he wanted to watch TV, but he also wanted to be there with me. The kids were going back and forth between houses easily by then, but sometimes just realizing a book or game was in the wrong house could set off a wave of emotion. He had also heard about the woman and her baby as well as the boy who had disappeared thirty years before. "Don't tell her," he said and pointed where his sister sat watching TV in the other room, her stuffed cat no longer recognizable as a cat, draped around her neck. He moved a little closer so he could hold his finger up for me to see and then leaned back, eyes closed, the glider moving in rhythm with his breath.

"A redhead has to take extra special care of her skin," Patrick's grandmother announced, people barely settled in for the first pitch. By now we all sat in the same places each time; mine was between Patrick's grandmother and the mother of the catcher, an accountant who sat and spent most of the time rifling through folders she brought in a big satchel. She was a redhead and fortunately had not yet arrived that day. "Feel mine? You see?" She extended her arm out to me and I obliged by rubbing a fingertip along her arm. "Jergens. A redhead has trouble aging well especially if she's skinny—no oils getting to that hair, dry as hay—she'd catch fire with one match like a piece of kindling. Speak of the devil." She laughed and nodded as the woman approached and then turned her attention to Marly and some of the other kids close by. "Hey, do you kids know the rules of good bathing?" she asked, and then proceeded to say in slow enunciated speech: "face, fanny, feet," pointing to her body parts as she sang. "Isn't that a good washcloth rule? If you know your alphabet you'll never forget the order." She pointed at Marly who was laughing but also by then holding tight to my arm. "She gets it. Smart girl. You'll never forget that will you? 'Face, fanny, feet.' Nobody should ever forget that. My mother taught me that long ago and I've been teaching it ever since."

Marly had told me that she was afraid of the old woman with the funny haircut, that she looked like the witch in *Hansel and Gretel*—a recent favorite of hers—which made me think of a little girl I'd once met when I was in college, a girl whose real life was sadly every bit as frightening. "The one that eats children," Marly added. She usually said these things at bedtime when she didn't want me to leave her room, the beg for just one more story, one more minute. It was hard not to try and imagine what the father from Delaware had told his daughter about her mom and baby brother and their leaving. *Leaving.* That's the way it was sometimes discussed, *leaving*, as if she had gotten in that Volvo and driven herself and her son out to the highway and was out there breathing in another part of the world. "Don't leave," Marly said and held my arm, so I stayed there beside her. Come morning she would be laughing and dancing around the kitchen singing *face, fanny, feet* like a jump rope rhyme, but not right then.

"Friend of mine's husband got some of that Viagra and she was in misery," Patrick's grandmother whispered. "He's near blind so I suggested she do a trick like what Jacob did to Esau, remember? Remember how he tricked his old blind daddy? I told my friend that's what she could do to her husband."

"How?" The man who asked this turned beet red but clearly couldn't help pursuing the topic.

"If you've got to ask, you don't deserve to know," she laughed, then added politely, "no offense."

"Frightening," the woman beside me said. "I wish she would be quieter."

"Okay then," Patrick's grandmother looked over and acted like she was zipping her lips. "It is frightening but so much of the Bible is, right? All that killing. It's a blood bath and what about that gal named something like Shazzam or something having to talk all the time so she won't be murdered."

"Well, I don't know much," the man offered. "But I know that what you're talking about is not from the Bible."

"Well," she pawed the air, "it's easy to get all that old stuff mixed up, isn't it? All of it scary stuff! Kids think they need chainsaws and murder, but truth is there is not much scarier than some Bible things—I saw all the movies—that big, bloody giant getting pelted in the head with rocks. Or people getting run down and killed by chariots." One little girl started crying and I was glad that Marly was over on the swings with the sister of the second baseman; an older girl who knew I would slip her a little money at the end of the game was watching them.

"You know what's scary?" she asked, more talkative than ever this day. Patrick's dad was not back by the fence as he normally was, and I wondered if something had happened. "Big doll babies that's what. I once had a dummy like Charlie What's-his-name but then I got scared of it—you know what I mean?" I knew exactly what she meant but I wasn't about to say anything. There were a lot of things that frightened me now that I was the only adult in the house. I no longer enjoyed reading or watching true crime or suspense as I once had. It seemed it might leak from the screen or page into the world I was creating. So I went with comedy and romance and nature shows. I closed shades to hold in the warm lamp light against the dark of winter.

"My friend, Sonia, once said what she was most afraid of was to get a physical, said she was scared bats would fly out, it had been so long since she'd had her legs spread like that. Bats! Isn't that funny?" Now there were two men listening, both blushing and trying not to laugh. "You think you're Batman? Is that it?" She turned on them and stared, two fingers crossed and sliding a silent *shame on you* before continuing. "Sonia said her car got serviced more often than she did."

* * *

One day, there was a father berating his kid, calling from the sidelines. He had done this at the few games he had attended and it was hard to watch, but no one was intervening. He stood there in tight white gym shorts and a tank top as if he was about to enter some kind of race, face red with his screams.

"And you can do it better, huh?" Patrick's grandmother called out. "Get on out there, Pete Rose, and show us then, *Big Boy*. Go on now, *Big Boy*." She stared hard. "You ought to be ashamed. Big man like you wanting to be even bigger." No one said anything, not even Patrick's dad, and she stared until the man, sensing we were all in agreement with her, turned and stormed over to the other side of the field, Patrick's grandmother whispering "good riddance."

We heard Patrick's mother was in hospice care and that other family members had begun to fly in for visits. I had even been part of a baking team though I had never met her; I left a casserole just inside their side storm door, lasagna steaming in the chilly night air. I had hoped Patrick's grandmother might hear me and come and say hello, but I didn't see anyone and chose not to ring the bell. Inside I could hear the sounds of Nickelodeon, the kind of normality we always take for granted, the normality I soothed myself in as I immersed my hands in that warm, sudsy water and stared into the dark woods.

Secretly, we were all happy about what Patrick's grandmother had said at the game, and for the rest of the season we called the man in the tight white shorts Big Boy behind his back. The redheaded accountant who it seemed was never paying attention had to excuse herself so she wouldn't laugh out loud. "That one needs some hair conditioner," Patrick's grandmother whispered to me as soon as she left. "She can't help it but it's true." I kept my eye trained on Marly across the schoolyard on the jungle gym and tire swing.

I found a reason to reach in my bag and while doing so, scooted my chair a little bit away, but by then she was already back with the ballgame, yelling for Patrick to hit it out of the park. This was the kind of day that left me most aware of the emptiness. The Big Boy story would have been one to tell over dinner, both of us laughing and appreciating something funny that had happened even if we were in the midst of breaking up and figuring out who got what. I could have told it and the conversation and laughter, and then the reality of Patrick's mother's illness would have allowed us—just for a second—to stand on a higher plane than the one most stand on when taking apart a home.

"Anybody here ever see *Birdman of Alcatraz*?"

I said that I had, years before. I'd seen *Birdman* and also *Escape from Alcatraz*, and it took a minute to untangle them in my mind. "Burt Lancaster, right?" And in the moment I had a flash of that small black-and-white television, foil on the rabbit ears, the comfortable pine-paneled den of my childhood.

"It started with a sparrow, one little sparrow," she said. "You know a sparrow is common as dirt, which is why there's that song about his eye being on one. God, I mean." She laughed. "He isn't just keeping up with the blue jays in other words," she said and nodded toward the horse woman with the Chanel bag. "Or the big woodpeckers like Big Boy."

The young mother beside me asked if I would hold her baby while she walked over to her car to make a call, and I reached for her. I always loved the chance to hold her, to feel the heft of those baby dimpled legs, the sweet soured smell of her hair.

"'Bye baby bunting, papa's gone a hunting,'" Patrick's grandmother sang and leaned in close. "Do people still sing that?" The baby calmed when she sang, big blue eyes staring out. The baby gummed her fist, smiled. "Or what about 'Kookaburro'? Lots of bird songs aren't there? 'Mockingbird.'" She leaned closer, eye to eye, and the baby got quiet staring back at her. "The carrier pigeon flies and delivers a message like Morse code, tap tap tap." She said in a singsong storytelling voice. "My daddy knew that from the navy—tap tap tap—and he told me the woodpeckers were talking to him and I believed it. For years I believed it. They put little bands on the birds' legs to track them, you know? The bird flies as it pleases—free and high—and at night it perches and tucks its little head up under its wing and coos and carries on." The baby stared back, smiling. "They ought to leave the city is what I say. All it would take is one pigeon with a vision and that pigeon might call himself Moses and say, 'Come on now, flock—let's head to the suburbs.' Why wouldn't they want to be out here with the river and that big mall with the cinema and popcorn, am I right?" She was looking into the baby's eyes, waiting as if she expected an answer, the little girl smiling and gripping her finger. "I'm a bird that flew as far north as my wings could carry," she said, "Oh yes, I did, you know I did, I got some old wings but I did it and I'll tell you who's really wise, and that's the old hoot owl. I've got a little play hoot owl that belongs to my little boy. You would love it, oh yes you would." The baby kicked her plump legs in delight.

I was relieved to see that Patrick's dad had arrived after all and was in his usual spot by the fence with the same man he always stood with. I was trying to come up with the right way to ask about his wife, to show concern without appearing nosy. Patrick's grandmother was making whistles and birdcalls, the baby's hands reaching for her face. She held out her hands for me to hand her over, and I did as I had done several times before. She bounced the baby gently and kept doing her sounds, coos and hoots and "Bob White, Bob White." She asked, "Who is Bob White?" Then she turned back to the smiling infant and told her that she deserved a bird named after her. "Pretty bird. Pretty bird."

Several years later, when I saw on the news that thousands of migrating birds had crashed into a Wal-Mart parking lot in Utah, I would think of that afternoon. Artificial light had drawn the birds into the snow-blanketed asphalt, the storm clouds over the lights making the parking lot look like water and a safe place to land. There in the moment—Patrick's grandmother doing birdcalls for the laughing baby—I was looking for the right way to ask about her daughter or daughter-in-law; I wanted to reach out to her. How was Patrick doing? How was *she* doing?

"My husband said pigeons were like a 'bunch of damn immigrants' and I hated that. I hated the way he hated. And, I like the pigeons," she was saying. "I bet Big Boy says things like that. I bet Big Boy thinks we ought to kill immigrants and such." She looked over at the men, but it was clear that I was the only one who had heard this. *Hush little baby don't say a word.* She had just begun to sing and was asking that I help her remember the words when I noticed a dog I didn't recognize near the swingset where Marly sat with another girl. The high school girl had her phone up to her ear and had walked over to the parking lot, her back to them. Marly was at that fearless age, ready to touch or reach out to anything and I had an uncomfortable feeling, a kind of sudden panic as I saw her see the dog and without another thought, I was up and moving toward her, ignoring Patrick's grandmother who was asking me what came after buying a diamond ring, a looking glass? Horse and cart? Marly was approaching the dog, calling to him, her hand outstretched; his ears were back and tail down, no collar or owner in sight. I called her name, but she kept moving in the direction of the dog. He had caught something and held it clenched in his teeth. The teenager was still facing the parking lot, the other girl swinging what seemed long, slow shadowed arcs; I heard the crack of a bat. Then there was a big commotion on the field, but I didn't turn, just kept moving forward to grab her. I fumbled in my purse for what I might throw, paint charts and a bag of popcorn, Evan's Game Boy. And then I moved faster and had her in my arms and the dog, maybe frightened by all the noise on the field, moved back in the direction of the shrubbery and woods. Marly was twisting to get away from me, angry that I had scared the dog away, and at the same time, I registered the high-pitched screams and turned to see one of the kids on the field wailing, his face bloody, and all the kids on their knees searching the grass for what I soon learned was the boy's front tooth. I scanned the crowd and breathed a small sigh of relief when I saw Evan's number 12 among those crouched and searching.

Marly was still struggling to get away and screaming about the dog and I heard one of the umpires say he didn't know if they would continue the game or not, but suspected they would once everyone settled back down. The sun was low in the sky by then, barely visible over the darkened school and the temperature had dropped just enough that people were reaching for their sweaters while waiting to see what would happen. I was almost back to my chair, my eye on the boy, who now had a towel up to his mouth and the coach rubbing his back; his mother—the horse woman—was on her phone, voice loud and near hysterical, calling their dentist to say they were on their way.

"Poor kid," I said to the young mother heading toward me and I finally let go of Marly with the promise she would stay right there.

"Where is she?" the woman asked. "Where is your mother?"

Her face filled with terror and in what seemed a long, horrible moment, I pictured *my* mother, seven hundred miles away in a nursing facility. Bingo. Cafeteria food. She had not been asked to sit at the popular table and my chest ached worse than it had thirty years before when I had said this same thing to her.

"My mother?"

"She was right here. You let her hold my baby!"

"That's not my mother."

"Oh God." The game was still stopped; it seemed everything stopped. "How could you?" The woman kept saying. *How could you?*

"She's Patrick's grandmother and his dad is right there." I pointed and looked at him, but he just shook his head slowly, confused that I ever would have thought such a thing. Several people called 911 but before anyone could even respond, we saw her crossing the street and coming back across the field, the baby in her arms. As she got closer, we saw that she also carried a stuffed owl, its glass eyes all scratched and patches of feathers missing. She was making owl sounds, *whoo whoo*, and the baby was laughing and reaching for her barrettes.

We learned that afternoon, once the police arrived, once the game that no one paid any attention to had ended, that she was not related to anyone at all but lived in a nearby facility. She had found a way in and out of the building without being detected, the bracelet banding her ankle and hidden by her thick socks defective. When one of the attendants came over to speak with us and explain what had happened and how it had happened, the young man assured us that she was harmless but that she was probably going to have to be moved to some place better equipped to keep her from roaming. He touched his head as he said this, gave a shrug. She had no local family, just a son in Canada who had visited only once.

"She has a lot of good stories," one of the fathers said, but we were quickly told that you couldn't believe a thing she said. And yet, I had believed a lot that she said. I had trusted her.

The rest of the season the spot beside me remained empty. She was missing, and then in another two weeks so were Patrick and his father. By the last game—warm breeze, pizza deliveries, kids excited about end of school and summer plans, the mood had thawed as well. Everyone got a trophy and we all said how we would look for each other when out and about town. The baby was cutting a tooth and her mother had allowed me to hold her once again, to breathe in that good baby smell. I had missed that and I had also missed the woman I thought was Patrick's grandmother, though I knew I was in the minority on that topic. As a group, we disagreed about many things: blue laws and taxes, religion, politics, yet we all shared the desire to keep our children safe. In that way, we were all together. The black sheet at the edge of town had disappeared and been replaced with a big yellow sun like a smiley face proclaiming *Happy Summer*—and up in the high branches of a tree in our yard, I saw a glint of silver, one single strand.

ACKNOWLEDGMENTS

I wish to thank the various magazines—and their editors and staff—that originally published some of the stories included. I am also grateful to Elizabeth Cox, Lee Smith, Cathy Stanley, and my sister, Jan Gane, for early readings and lifelong encouragement..

I thank Shannon Ravenel, to whom this book is dedicated and who was my editor for thirty years. I learned so much from her and am eternally grateful for the experience and her lasting guidance.

Thanks to those who made this book happen: my agent Henry Dunow and the whole Algonquin team: Brunson Hoole, Ashley Mason, Debra Linn, Travis Smith, Anna Skudlarek,

Cathy Schott (I love this jacket!), Stephanie Mendoza, Michael McKenzie, and Betsy Gleick. A big thanks to Chris Stamey and Abigail Pugh for their attentive copyediting and proofreading.

An abundance of gratitude to my editor, Kathy Pories, whom I am honored to work with, and whose generous insights are a marvel.

Thanks to my colleagues and students in the Bennington Writing Seminars (shout-out to the Dog House and the many inhabitants over the years!) and to Arlene Robinson and Rascal, who make an appearance in this collection as result of their very generous donation to the Gloucester-Mathews Humane Society.

And finally, thanks as always to my husband, Tom Rankin, for his steadfast love and support, and our shared family. I thank Claudia and Rob, who will always be my greatest source of pride and inspiration, and Ashlee, who has been family from the start.